ROGER MARCHAM'S WARD.

ROGER MARCHAM'S WARD.

Roger Marcham's Ward

By

ANNIE S. SWAN

Author of "Across Her Path," "Aldersyde," &c.

Edinburgh and London

Oliphant, Anderson and Ferrier

Books by Annie S. Swan.

3s. 6d.

Sheila. With Frontispiece.
Maitland of Laurieston. *A Family History.* With Frontispiece.
The Gates of Eden. *A Story of Endeavour.* With Portrait of the
    Authoress.
Briar and Palm. *A Study of Circumstance and Influence.* With
    Frontispiece.
St. Veda's. With Frontispiece by Robert M'Gregor.
The Guinea Stamp. *A Tale of Modern Glasgow.*
Who Shall Serve? *A Story for the Times.*
A Lost Ideal.

2s. 6d.

Aldersyde. Frontispiece.
Carlowrie. Frontispiece.
Hazell and Sons. Illustrated.
A Divided House. Illustrated.
Ursula Vivian. Illustrated.
The Ayres of Studleigh. Frontispiece.
Doris Cheyne. With Illustrations of the English Lake District.

Cloth, 1s. 6d. Illustrated.

Across Her Path.
A Divided House. Cheap Edition.
Sundered Hearts.
Robert Martin's Lesson.
Mistaken, and Marion Forsyth.
Shadowed Lives.
Ursula Vivian. Cheap Edition.
Dorothea Kirke.
Life to those that are Bound.
Wrongs Righted.
The Secret Panel.
Thomas Dryburgh's Dream, and Miss Baxter's Bequest.
Twice Tried.
A Vexed Inheritance.
Hazell and Sons. Cheap Edition.
A Bachelor in Search of a Wife.
Aldersyde. Cheap Edition.
Doris Cheyne. Cheap Edition.
Carlowrie. Cheap Edition.
The Bonnie Jean, and other Stories.

Cloth, 1s.

Airlie's Mission. Illustrated.
The Bonnie Jean. Illustrated.
St. Veda's.

Paper Covers, 6d.

St. Veda's; or, The Pearl of Orr's Haven.

LORIMER AND CHALMERS, PRINTERS, EDINBURGH.

CONTENTS.

ROGER MARCHAM'S WARD.

CHAPTER I.

UNCLE AND NEPHEW.

WHAT on earth shall we do with her?"

"Do with whom, Uncle Roger?"

"This girl, Dorothy Vance, my old friend Geoffrey Vance's daughter Dorothy. She is on her way here, and will arrive soon; in fact she should be in London to-night or to-morrow."

"Oh, Jerusalem!" was the intelligent comment of the younger of the two gentlemen, and he grinned as he carefully cut the top from his third egg, and poured out another cup of coffee for himself.

He was a good-looking young fellow, of the foppish type, with close-cropped hair, carefully-pointed moustache, high-pointed collar, and immaculate boots. Fred Wellesley had a very high opinion of himself. The other occupant of the room, Roger Marcham, Squire of Underwood, presented a fine contrast to his insignificant-looking nephew. He was a man in his full prime, and carried a splendid figure and noble head set on a pair of broad, manly shoulders.

His dark hair was slightly tinged with grey, as was the short, pointed beard so becoming to his face. His deep, dark eye was kind and keen and true; looking into it you felt at once that Roger Marcham was a man to be trusted—ay, to the uttermost limit that human trust can go. He seemed perplexed by the letter he had just received, and the contents of which he had communicated to his nephew in an exclamation of surprise.

"But what's she coming here for?" queried Fred Wellesley, with his mouth full. "Underwood isn't quite the place for young lady visitors, is it?"

"No, but she is not coming here as a visitor, but as a permanent resident. Miss Vance will make her home at Underwood," said Roger Marcham, not without a certain reserve of manner.

"Phew! Mystery on mystery! Why should she make her home here? Has she any claim on you?"

"Yes, her father and I were brothers in every thing but name," returned Roger Marcham, briefly. "I promised when I was in India eight years ago, that, in case of anything happening to him, I would take care of his only child. He has died suddenly, it seems, and of course my promise requires fulfilment."

"Very good of you, I'm sure, Uncle Roger; you're charitable to every one but yours truly," drawled Fred Wellesley. "But if this little Indian is up to anything, she'll enliven Underwood for a fellow. It's dull enough as it is."

"You are too fond of it as it is, Fred. I only wish it saw less of you and the office more," said the elder man, candidly. "You have no business to be idling your time here just now."

"Oh, hang it! Couldn't stay in town after the 12th. Only barbarians do it," said Fred, languidly. "Let a fellow alone, and he'll go up and work no end after a fortnight's shooting. Any common clerk has that now-a-days."

"You have too many holidays, Fred, and I'm going to take sharper measures with you, my lad," said his uncle, quietly. "But to return to Miss Vance. You must go up to London and meet her, Fred. I have two meetings to-day, from which I cannot absent myself. Can I trust you to do this without making a fool of yourself?"

"Oh, come now, draw it mild," said Fred, with an assumption of offended dignity. "Remember a fellow's a gentleman, at any rate."

Roger Marcham laughed.

"One thing I must ask of you, Fred, not to speak so much slang before Miss Vance. It is offensive to me, and I do not wish my ward's ears to be offended in the like manner. There are plenty of words in the English language without coining them for yourself."

"I'm not going to make a prig of myself, even though Miss Vance's ears should be offended," retorted the young man with a touch of sulkiness. "If she doesn't like the way I speak, she needn't listen."

"I shall require you to obey me, my lad, while you are at Underwood," said Roger Marcham, quietly, but firmly; "and I shall expect you to remember my hint. Well, will you go up and meet Miss Vance?"

"If I'm to obey you, I suppose I must," said

Fred, kicking the table leg more like a sulky school-boy than a man of three-and-twenty. "Where is she coming from, and how shall I know her?"

"She is a passenger in the *Indus*, and is due to-day. You must ask for Miss Vance, and if she is not too tired, come down to Norton by the first train. Send a telegram, if not, so that Kennard may have the carriage at the station."

"Very well; and am I to shut up all the time, because I can't promise that I won't talk slang? But perhaps Miss Vance may be a jolly girl, who rather likes things off-hand, and talks slang herself."

"I scarcely think it; and I sincerely hope not," returned Roger Marcham. "Well, I must go now. If you make haste, you will catch the 10.55. I should not like the poor girl to arrive in London and find no one meeting her. She will be downhearted and lonely enough as it is."

"I hope she isn't one of the weeping willows," said Fred, shrugging his shoulders; "because I can't condole, you know. I believe in taking things easily. A short life and a merry one, is my creed."

"Some day soon I think you will awaken to the reality of life, my boy," said Roger Marcham, a trifle sadly. "I wish something would rouse you. I am often anxious about you. There is only a step between idleness and sin, if indeed idleness is not a sin."

"Oh, draw it mild," said Fred, taking his legs from between the table, and rising indolently to his feet. "Don't make a fellow out a weed until he *is* one. I don't drink, or bet, or do anything very bad."

"You haven't even sufficient energy to do anything with all your might. I think if you had been left to your own resources, you would have made a man of yourself long ago."

"Well, it isn't very nice to throw what you have done for a fellow into a fellow's face," said the young man, complainingly. "And I'm sure I work jolly hard in that wretched old office for my beggarly pittance. I'm no better treated than any other clerk. Not one of the fellows I know would take it so easily."

If Mr. Fred Wellesley's pittance was so beggarly, where did the diamond horseshoe in his breastpin and the flashing brilliants on his little finger come from? To look at Mr. Wellesley, one would not have thought he supported himself on a beggarly pittance. His uncle's attire presented a curious contrast to his; but it was not difficult to determine which was the more perfect gentleman.

"There is no use arguing this vexed question, Fred. It is one on which you and I need never hope to agree, until you gather common sense. But don't forget that I have left you at perfect liberty to leave our establishment, if you think you can better yourself elsewhere."

"Now, that's mean. After bringing up a fellow like a gentleman, to tell a fellow he can go and mix with cads," said the aggrieved Fred. "I'm your only relation in the world, and you should do something handsome for me. What are you going to do with all your money if you don't give me a share?"

Roger Marcham's colour rose slightly. Perhaps the young man presumed a little. He was his only sister's son, but even that tie would not excuse such a speech. He made no reply, but turned quickly on his heel and left the room. Sometimes Roger Marcham's nephew was a sore trial to him. He had no patience with the indolence and lack of manly independence displayed by Fred Wellesley. These qualities had no part in Roger Marcham's character, else he had never attained to such an honoured and responsible position. With his own energy and untiring industry he had built up the business house of Marcham, Marcham & Co., until it was a magnificent concern, yielding an immense return. But though now a very rich man, Roger Marcham had not abated a jot of his early industry. If he did not now sit on a stool in his own counting-house, the entire concern was still under his own supervision. Then he had numerous other duties devolving upon him as the master of a considerable estate in the country. He had undertaken various responsibilities in connection with County affairs, which he faithfully fulfilled, and it was his endeavour to make himself acquainted with the circumstances and requirements of all the people on his lands. It could not be said, therefore, that Roger Marcham led an idle life. But he loved to be in the midst of work; it was the wine of life to him. Many wondered why one so honoured and esteemed, so well fitted in every way to build up a happy home, which would be a centre of sweet influences, should live so solitary a life. If there was any past romance, any page of his young history which might have accounted for it, it was not known. Roger Marcham was kind, courteous, chivalrous towards all women, but paid particular attention to none. He had evidently

"The Squire of Underwood cantered into Norton that
fine autumn morning."

not yet met the woman he could ask to share his heart and home. This being so, Fred Wellesley, the child of Roger Marcham's only sister, who had made an imprudent marriage with a worthless man, was regarded as his uncle's sole heir. Perhaps this knowledge or assumption was at the root of the youth's idle habits and calm presuming on his relative's kind nature, but Roger Marcham preferred to believe that Fred had inherited weaknesses to struggle against. Sometimes the lad's failings lay heavy on his heart, and he was utterly perplexed as to what course he should pursue with him.

As the Squire of Underwood cantered into Norton that fine autumn morning, however, his thoughts were not occupied with his nephew. Memory was busy in his heart, recalling old scenes, old faces, old experiences, which sent a warm thrill through his whole being. He had loved Geoffrey Vance with a brother's love. Together they had sat on one bench at school and college; together they had entered on life's battle, and were fighting with equal success when Geoffrey Vance's health failed, and he was obliged to sail, with his wife and child, to the shores of that distant land which had given him and his darling a grave. Roger Marcham's heart was filled with sympathy and sorrow for the young girl, orphaned in a foreign land, coming over the sea to seek a home with unknown and untried friends. He had never seen the child. When making a business visit to Calcutta, Geoffrey Vance had travelled hundreds of miles from his inland home to meet with the friend of his youth. He was a broken-down man then, with the shadow of an early death on his heart, and

Roger Marcham had gladly given the promise to take care of his friend's child as soon, and so long, as she required his care.

Now that she was so near that a few hours would bring her to Underwood, Roger Marcham felt a trifle anxious and perplexed. It had come upon him so suddenly that he could make no arrangements; she must just take them as they were, and depend, for a time at least, on the motherly kindness of the old housekeeper, who was as much part of Underwood as its master; and then, counting up the years, Roger Marcham was amazed and a trifle dismayed to find that Dorothy Vance must be twenty-one. So it was a young lady, and not a child, he had to welcome home—a grave responsibility for a man who knew nothing about women, their ways, and needs.

"There's no use worrying over it," he said to himself, trying to fling off the apprehension he felt stealing over him. "Child or woman, I must do the best I can for her, for her father's sake."

So he resolved, not dreaming how very soon he would account it the highest privilege in the world to do the best for her, for her own sweet sake.

CHAPTER II.

DOROTHY VANCE.

ROGER MARCHAM attended a meeting of Guardians in Norton, lunched at the Norton Arms, and rode on to be present at a County meeting in Midgate. It was a protracted affair, and the afternoon was well spent before it terminated. It would take him all his time to be home for the six o'clock dinner.

He had given the County affairs only a divided attention, his mind being occupied with thoughts of the stranger coming to his home. He was conscious of a curious feeling of excitement as he rode through his own gates that fine evening. As he watched the shafts of sunlight piercing the leafy boughs of the beeches which were the pride of Underwood, he wondered whether Dorothy Vance would admire them.

"Do you know if the carriage went to the station, Mrs. Curtis?" he asked the lodge-keeper.

"Yes, sir, to meet the half-past four train. It has just gone back about ten minutes ago."

"With Mr. Fred and a young lady?"

"Yes, sir," the woman answered, and he saw that her curiosity was aroused.

"We are to have a new experience at Underwood, Mrs. Curtis. The young lady is my ward, just returned from India. She will make her home here, at least for a time," said the Squire. "We must all try and make her as happy as we can. She has had a great deal of sorrow, and has just lost the best father any girl ever had."

"Indeed, sir. Poor dear. She's as sweet-lookin' a cretur' as ever I saw, sir, an' a real lady as ever I saw, sir, by the way she holds her head. It'll make a bit o' a change in the Hall, sir."

"Ay, it will," returned the Squire; and with a nod and a smile rode on. It was twenty minutes to six when he handed the reins to the groom at the door, and hurried into the house.

On the stairs he met Fred, in immaculate evening dress, whereat his uncle stared in amazement.

"Hulloa, what's this for?"

"For Miss Vance, of course. It's all very well to sit down to one's feed in blue serge when there's only fellows, but when there's a lady in the house it's different. She's a stunner, Uncle Roger."

Roger Marcham smiled.

"You must have had very little time to spare in London?"

"Only an hour and a half. I was just in time for the *Indus*, so I took Miss Vance to the Continental for a bit of lunch, and then we came on."

"You did well. Where is she now?"

"Oh, upstairs; old Maple waiting on her hand and foot. Shouldn't wonder, Uncle Roger, if the fair Indian usurps your place here. She looks as if she'd been accustomed to homage all her days—by Jove! she does. She was rather stand-offish with yours truly at first, but she seemed to find out after a bit that I wasn't a half bad fellow. We are tip-top friends now."

' That's right, Fred," laughed Roger Marcham as he ran upstairs, hugely amused by the young fellow's conceit.

In an incredibly short time Roger Marcham had dressed, and was descending to the drawing-room, when the opening of a door near him caused him to look round. When he saw a girlish figure coming along the corridor he retraced his steps, and they met just at the painted window on the landing."

"Dorothy Vance, my friend's child. You are welcome to Underwood," he said, and took the slim, pale hands in his firm, warm grasp, and, bending forward, touched the low, broad forehead with his lips.

"My guardian, Uncle Roger, papa said I was to call you," she said, with a strange wistfulness. Her large grey eyes dwelt for a moment searchingly on his face, and Roger Marcham stood in silence, feeling that she was only seeking to know in that first long look how it was to be between them. Her colour rose a little, he felt her hands tremble, and a sweet smile touched her proud, womanly mouth. "I think I have come home," was all she said, but the words were the sweetest in the world to Roger Marcham's heart.

"Sit down here just for a moment, my dear," he said, drawing her to the low window seat. "Before we go down just let me tell you how glad I am to think I can fulfil my promise to your father. Geoffrey Vance's daughter and

Geoffrey Vance's chum can never be like strangers to each other."

"Oh no, I am so glad you are like what you are," she said, with a swift, ingenuous smile. "I got such a fright on the quay to-day, fearing your nephew was yourself."

Roger Marcham laughed, and that laugh was a pleasant sound to hear. Then a little silence fell upon them, for Roger Marcham's thoughts bore a curious mingling of regret over the past, and much up-springing of hopes for the future. He could scarcely believe that this tall, slight, self-possessed young lady, with the grave, sweet, womanly face, crowned by its glossy brown hair, could verily be the child of his old friend. It seemed but yesterday since they were boys together, building castles in the air, and planning for themselves a glorious future of achievement and endeavour. And what were the thoughts of Dorothy Vance? She had come over the sea in obedience to her father's last request, leaving behind the only friends she had ever known, to trust herself with the unknown comrade her father had loved so well. She had formed many ideas of what Roger Marcham would be like, but when her eyes fell upon that noble face, with its grave charm of expression, and kindly, honest eye, every apprehension fled, and a strange feeling of rest and trust stole into her heart. She felt, indeed, as she expressed it, that she had come home.

"Shall we go down, now?" said Roger Marcham, offering his arm. "Dinner will be served now, and Fred impatient. I hope he did his duty. It was a great disappointment to me that I could not meet you myself. But the letter only came to-day, and I could not put off my engagements."

"Certainly not. Mr. Wellesley was most kind and attentive. I am afraid I shall be a great trouble to you, Mr. Marcham."

"In what way?"

"Oh, girls are always troublesome. Papa told me I was to do all I could to make you happy, and I will."

"Thank you. If you feel happy and at home at Underwood, Dorothy, I shall be happy," said Roger Marcham, sincerely. "You will find a great deal needing your attention, I am afraid. We are very Bohemian in our habits."

"Does Mr. Wellesley live here always?"

"He ought not. He is supposed to have work to do in the office," returned Roger Marcham, and said no more, as they had reached the dining-room door.

Fred Wellesley was in his element that night. Roger Marcham was amused by his evident desire to carry the heart of the stranger by storm. Roger himself said very little, and left the young people to carry on the conversation, which they did without a break. He was pleased to see that Fred seemed anxious to be as gentlemanly as possible, and that he refrained from the use of slang, which was a great concession. Miss Vance seemed to be an accomplished talker, and she was quick at repartee. When once a sweet, clear trill of laughter sounded through the sombre old room, Roger Marcham almost started at the unusual sound.

"Won't you come out for a stroll, Miss Vance?" said Fred, eagerly, the moment dinner

was over.   "Uncle Roger always has letters to
write, and we 'll just be in the way."

Roger Marcham bit his lip, but turned to his
ward with a smile.

"Yes, if you are not too tired, go with Fred
through the park.   Can I get a wrap for you?"

"Won't you come too?" she asked, with a
slight hesitation, which he misunderstood.

"Oh, no, an old fogey like me might be in the
way," he said, with a laugh.   "When Fred goes
back to town you will have plenty of time to
weary of me."

So Fred had his way, and they left the house
together, Roger Marcham watching them from
the window with a slight cloud upon his brow.
Well, perhaps it was but natural and right that
he should be set aside.   He was old and grey
and grave, and could have nothing in common
with those just standing on life's threshold.
He was only "Uncle Roger," and of what use
in the world is an uncle but to provide the means
for the young people to spend, and stand aside
while they enjoy it.   And yet he felt impatient
of his nephew's appropriation of Dorothy Vance;
on this first night, at least, he might have kept
in the background ; he might have thought that
guardian and ward would have something to say
to each other, if only to speak about those who
were gone.   No such consideration, however,
had presented itself to the mind of Mr. Fred
Wellesley.   He was seized with a sudden and
boundless admiration for Miss Vance, and, in
accordance with his usual selfishness, claimed
her society without giving his uncle a thought.
It had been understood that a fortnight was to
be the limit of the young man's autumn holidays,

but the fortnight came and went, and another began to draw to a close, without any sign that Fred was wearying to get back to work. At length Roger Marcham deemed it his duty to speak.

He found him idly smoking a cigar on the terrace one afternoon, and walking up to him, said, candidly—

"You must turn up at the office on Monday morning, Fred. I have waited this time to see how far you would transgress the bounds of what is reasonable and right."

He spoke quietly, but he was gravely displeased. Fred, however, only replied by a flippant laugh.

"All right, gov. I'll go up on Monday, but I was going to say I think I'll run down always on Friday nights, and stay till Monday all winter."

"There are two to agree on that question, Fred," returned his uncle, quietly. "If you do so, you must pay for your short time, if only as an example to the rest."

"Oh, come, that would be too mean on a fellow, I declare. You're getting worse every day. Uncle Roger, what's the use of being so hard on a fellow?"

"Hard, my lad; I am not hard enough."

"I don't know what you call hard, then? Haven't I seen you scowling at me for a week back, but I was bound I wouldn't give in. I'm not to be treated as if I were a common cad. You promised long ago, you know, to make me like your own son. You can't go back on it now."

"I promised to put you in a fair way of earn-

ing your own livelihood. If you imagine by that
that I intended to hand over the entire fruits of
my life's labour to a man who had never learned
the value of an honestly-earned shilling, you
were under a mistake, Fred, and the sooner you
know it the better."

"Oh, hang it! draw it mild. What are you
driving at. Do you want me to quit?"

"I'll tell you what I want, and what I will
have, Fred, or you and I must part. You must
go back to business, and apply yourself to learn
its principles, of which you are curiously ignorant
even yet. You must make yourself of some use
in the place, or it cannot hold you. Your example
is pernicious in its effects on the others, and,
unless it is amended, must be removed."

Fred Wellesley threw away the end of his
cigar in a passion.

"It's only since Miss Vance came you've
grown so mighty anxious about me," he said,
bitterly.

"I see you doing your utmost to win the
affections of my ward, Fred," said Roger
Marcham, with quiet dignity, "and, as she is in
my care, I must see to it that the man who
seeks to win her is worthy of her. You are not
so. Until you make a man of yourself, Fred,
I fear I must banish you from Underwood—
I must speak plainly. It is my duty to myself,
to you, and to her."

"Then I'd better get out to-night," said
Fred, bitterly, and a scowl darkened his brow.
"I must say it's a pretty way to treat a fellow,
and I won't forget it."

So saying, Mr. Fred Wellesley made haste
into the house, got up to his dressing-room,

gathered his things together, and prepared to make off to the station. He was rather pleased on the whole to be able to pose as a hero and a martyr. He hoped for an opportunity to show himself in his new *role* to Miss Vance, and he was not disappointed. As he left the house he met her on the terrace, with a wrap round her head, and her hands full of autumn leaves.

"Oh, Mr. Wellesley, where are you going?" she asked, glancing in amazement at his portmanteau.

"London. The gov.'s kicked me out. He says I can't live on charity any longer. A pretty thing to have thrown in a fellow's teeth, eh?"

"I don't believe he said such a thing. If I were your gov., as you call him, I'd have sent you off long ago," was the unexpected and candid rejoinder. "I never met any one so lazy and idle as you. Have you any aim in life?"

"Yes, I have now, and, by Jove, I'll win it, too," said Fred Wellesley, with astonishing energy. "Neither you nor the gov. need flatter yourselves you've got rid of me, because you haven't."

So saying, Mr. Fred stalked away, and Dorothy Vance went into the house with a smile of amusement on her lips. It changed to one of grave tenderness, however, as she paused for a moment in the pillared doorway, and looked out on the peace and beauty of the autumn night. What tender thought had touched her heart, and brought a sudden dimness to her eyes? She turned about presently, and, crossing the hall, opened the library door and looked in. Roger Marcham was sitting at a table with papers and

writing materials before him, his face wearing an
anxious and troubled look. Dorothy Vance
entered and gently closed the door.

"May I come in for a moment, Mr. Marcham?
I shall not disturb you long."

"Surely, come in, come in!"

She advanced to the table and laid her many-
coloured leaves upon it. He wondered why her
hands trembled, and the sweet colour flitted so
restlessly in her cheek.

"Fred has gone away, I believe," he said,
with a half smile. "It will be very dull at
Underwood for you now."

"Why now?" she asked, nervously fingering
the leaves, and keeping her sweet eyes down-
cast.

"Because you have no one to enliven the
place for you."

"*You* are not going away?" she said, lifting
her eyes suddenly to his face.

"No."

She nodded gravely, and then walking over to
the window stood for a moment looking out
into the gathering darkness. Roger Marcham
looked at the graceful outline of her figure
showing against the window, and wondered why
his heart should be filled with such strange
unrest. Dorothy Vance had not brought peace
from over the sea, and yet her presence had
brought an unwonted sunshine into Underwood.
Roger Marcham knew already that it would be
empty without her.

"I have been thinking, Dorothy," he said, in
his grave, quiet manner, "that perhaps it isn't
quite a good thing for a young girl like you to
be so much alone, to have no companionship

but mine. If you like, I shall set about getting
a lady companion to reside here."

"I do not need a companion, Mr. Marcham.
I have Rosamond Tracy when I am dull," she
answered, in a low voice, and without turning
her head. The next moment she came forward
to the table, and, leaning her slim hand on it,
looked at him with an exquisite blending of shy-
ness and wistful tenderness.

"I know I am a great trouble to you," she
said. "But I shall try not to be in your way.
I need no companion. I am happy in having
so beautiful a home, so kind a guardian. Will
you let things go on as they have been since
I came, and I shall try not to be in your way?"

The colour rose in Roger Marcham's cheek.
How she had misunderstood him! He restrained
himself by a mighty effort. He did not know
what possessed him, but he felt towards this
sweet girl as he never felt towards any woman.
Could it be that thus late in life love had come
to him, to make havoc of his peace of mind?

"Very well, my dear," he said, in tones which
his great effort made cold and calm. "We
shall just let things go on in the meantime.
You are not in my way, and I am glad you feel
yourself at home in Underwood."

CHAPTER III.

RIVALS.

"BUT mamma, it is impossible we can ask Mr. Marcham without Dorothy Vance," said Rosamond Tracy. "It would look most extraordinary."

"Why? We used to ask Mr. Marcham before his ward appeared. Why not now?" asked Mrs. Tracy, sharply. "I don't like Dorothy Vance, Rosamond, and I'm not going to pretend I do."

"Why don't you like her, my dear?" asked the Vicar, a mild, gentle-hearted man, much under the control of his clever, ambitious wife. "I am sure she is a very sweet girl."

"Oh, I am sick of hearing her called a sweet girl," retorted Mrs. Tracy. "Were I a strong young woman like her I would rather toil night and day than live on Roger Marcham's charity."

Mrs. Tracy was not a lady, as her manner and speech and expression indicated. The Vicar looked nervous and put out.

"My dear, you should not speak like that. Miss Vance is not altogether dependent on Mr. Marcham," he said, quickly. "I hope you have never said anything of the kind outside. Mr. Marcham only told me that Mr. Vance had left very little. He also said that his ward did not know. He gave me these items in confidence, and I ought not to have betrayed it."

"I am not likely to speak of it outside," was all the satisfaction his wife deigned to give. Then she turned once more to her daughter, who was busy writing invitations at the davenport— "Do you really think, then, that we must include Dorothy Vance?"

"Yes, I do."

"Most certainly," put in the Vicar, and considerably relieved, he left the room.

"It was the most unfortunate thing in the world that Dorothy Vance should have come here just when she did," said Mrs. Tracy, rather complainingly. "I am quite sure that Mr. Marcham was just on the point of speaking last autumn. He was never out of the house."

"It was papa he came to see," said Rosamond, quietly.

"Oh, nonsense! He admired you very much. He told me so, often."

"He might admire me. I daresay he did," said Rosamond, a trifle absently, and her eyes wandered over the sunny landscape to the green woods surrounding Roger Marcham's home. But she was not thinking of him. Rosamond Tracy was a handsome girl, and one possessed of a strong will and determination. It was her mother's ambition to make a splendid match for her; and she had fixed on Roger Marcham as the most desirable. But on this point Rosamond and she did not agree.

"No doubt Dorothy Vance thinks it would be a very fine thing to be mistress of Underwood," said Mrs. Tracy, rather vindictively.

"I am quite sure, mother, that Dorothy has

never thought of such a thing. I never saw a girl of her years less worldly wise," said Rosamond. She was not particularly amiable nor charitable as a rule in her judgment of others, but in this instance she was just to Dorothy Vance.

" 'You are infatuated with the girl. I think her deep and scheming," said Mrs. Tracy. "If she wins your best chance away from you, what will you say ? "

"If you mean Roger Marcham, mamma, she is welcome to him," she replied, calmly. "Well, how am I to word the invitation to Underwood ? Is Fred Wellesley to be included ? "

"We must send him an invitation, of course, but you had better address it to the office," said Mrs. Tracy, readily. "If he comes, Miss Vance will be disposed of for the whole afternoon. I hear he is quite infatuated with her."

Rosamond's brow darkened, her lip trembled, and a bitter look crossed her face as she took the pen in her hand. Unconsciously her mother had given her a cruel sting. Strange as it may seem, Rosamond Tracy had given her strong heart into Fred Wellesley's keeping. What had been a summer's idle pastime to him had been earnest for her. She was capable of a deep, passionate affection, and she had given it to Roger Marcham's nephew, a man who had never given a serious thought to anything in his life. Never until he met Dorothy Vance.

"These three will make twenty, mamma," she said, quietly. "That is quite enough. Our tennis ground is not too big, and there is no use crowding the grounds."

"No, no, that is quite enough. I do not give

many parties, but I flatter myself that they are always enjoyable and select—my garden parties especially so," said Mrs. Tracy, with a self-complacency which made her daughter smile.

The invitations were all accepted, for, to do Mrs. Tracy justice, her entertainments were always enjoyable and well-appointed. The party from Underwood were a little late, having waited for Fred to come down by the noon train. He had applied himself to business so well of late that Roger Marcham was much pleased. It made him rejoice that he had at last awakened to his responsibility, and yet sometimes a little dissatisfaction mingled with and marred the elder man's gladness, for the cause was very apparent. Dorothy Vance's influence had wrought the change, and there was no doubt in Roger Marcham's mind as to the issue. There were times when he wished his ward had remained in that far country. She had made Underwood too bright a place with her gracious presence. What would it be without it now?

Opinion in Norton was divided as to Roger Marcham's ward. She was not popular in the ordinary sense of the word; her reticent, shy manner was taken for pride, she could not make herself frank and pleasant to all, and she had a natural shrinking from strangers; but those who had seen most of her were astonished to find that she began to creep into their hearts. She was perfectly unaffected, and, when occasion offered, fearless in her upholding of the right and condemnation of the wrong—too much so for the conventional ideas of certain folk in Norton, but Roger Marcham would not have had her different in one particular for worlds. He loved

to see her eye grow moist, her smile, sweet
and tender, when a generous deed was done or
spoken of; he admired the kindling flash, the
heightened colour with which she spoke of what
was mean and ignoble; she had exalted ideas of
life, her ideal was high and pure and true.
Little did Roger Marcham dream that he was
her ideal of all that was best in manhood.   Like
all fine natures, he had a humble opinion of his
own merits; often he was weighed down by the
thought that his society was irksome to her, that
the tie between guardian and ward was one she
would gladly break.   He thought it would cost
her no effort to leave Underwood, that she
would gladly share his nephew's lot in life.
But these thoughts made no difference in his
manner towards her.   It was like that of a
father—grave, kind, considerate, solicitous for
her comfort in little things as well as great.
They were very happy together in their quiet
way, and yet there was a kind of restraint
between them; a misunderstanding on one
essential point.

Those who did not like Miss Vance refused to
admit that she was to be admired for her per-
sonal appearance, and yet it was impossible not
to be struck by the winning charm of her girlish
beauty as she entered the grounds that afternoon
by her guardian's side.   More than one thought
involuntarily that they looked a handsome, well-
matched pair.

"How do you do, Mr. Marcham?   So glad to
see you," said Mrs. Tracy, coming fussily across
the lawn to meet them.   "Ah, Mr. Wellesley,
delighted to see you also; so good of you to
come all the way from London to adorn this

33   C

"The two girls were good friends."

humble gathering. Ah, Miss Vance, how do you do?"

The difference in her greeting to Dorothy Vance annoyed Roger Marcham beyond measure. Dorothy herself was quite unconscious of it. She did not like the Vicar's wife, and seeing Rosamond approaching, she left her guardian's side and went on to meet her. The two girls were good friends, and without being aware of it, Dorothy had read Miss Tracy many a lesson. One thing, however, Rosamond would find it difficult to forgive her, and that was winning Fred Wellesley's allegiance away from her. And yet there was no trace of any such feeling visible in expression or manner, and she welcomed her rival with a smile and a kiss, though she had seen Fred Wellesley's open admiration for his uncle's ward visible in his manner as they crossed the lawn together.

"Good afternoon, Mr. Wellesley," she said, gaily, giving him her hand with the utmost indifference. "You truant, you have quite deserted Underwood. Is he not becoming a model business man, Dorothy?"

"Yes, and we are very proud and glad," smiled Dorothy. "Don't you think it is a change for the better?"

These words were to Fred Wellesley sufficient reward for the self-denial of the last few months. It was some plainly-uttered words which fell inadvertently from Dorothy Vance's lips which had shown him that to please her he must turn over a new leaf; naturally it was a satisfaction to him to be told, and thus publicly, that his efforts were not unappreciated.

"I suppose a fellow must do something some

time," he said rather tamely, but the look he
bent on Dorothy made Rosamond Tracy's heart
beat angrily. "Well, Miss Tracy, and how has
the world been using you?"

"As well as could be expected," she retorted,
a trifle sharply. "Dorothy, there is papa looking for you. You are a great favourite with
him."

Dorothy turned, and went up the path a little
to meet the Vicar, and Fred Wellesley and
Rosamond were left a moment alone.

"I haven't seen you looking so charming for
a long time, Rosamond," he said, the old temptation to flatter a pretty woman coming uppermost. "Upon my honour, you do look stun-
ning!"

Rosamond Tracy's colour rose, and she bit
her lip.

"Don't trouble to talk such rubbish to me,"
she said, haughtily.

"Oh, come now. We used to be such
friends. You haven't thrown me over, have you,
Rosamond?" he said, impressively.

Dorothy was out of sight, and for a moment
his old admiration for Rosamond Tracy returned.

"Thrown you over?" she repeated, slowly,
and lifted her passionate eyes to his face.

"You are mad with me, Rosamond," he said,
in that indolent way which to any high-spirited
woman would have been most offensive. "Let's
have a stroll by-and-by and talk it over. Could
you come now?"

"No. I must go and see if they are going to
play," she said. "If the sets can be made up
without me, I shall stay out."

So saying she walked away, and Fred turned to look for Dorothy. But the Vicar had claimed her, and carried her off to his favourite rockeries, where he was exhibiting some of his latest treasures in the shape of rock plants.

Much to Fred's disappointment, he found no opportunity for a quiet talk with Dorothy. She seemed to have come out of her shell wonderfully, and was quite a centre of attraction at the cluster of garden chairs under the acacia tree. Rosamond's attention was taken up at the tea-table, and the liveliest part of the proceedings was nearly over before she was at liberty. While the guests were all busy with tea or ices, strolling about under the shadow of the trees, and making merry over the rival successes of the games, Rosamond, under the pretence of returning to the house, slipped through the shrubbery into the little park where the Vicarage ponies were enjoying the sunshine. She was leaning over the gate, caressing the petted pair, when she heard a footstep behind her. She did not look round, but her colour rose and her eyes betrayed the exultation in her heart.

"I thought you'd be here," said Fred Wellesley's voice. "Will you let a fellow finish his cigar here, Rosamond?"

"If you like," she answered, indifferently.

He sat up on the gate and looked down at the handsome figure in its perfectly fitting tennis dress, at the finely-featured face, shaded by the broad sun-hat. The hand resting on the pony's glossy neck was white and exquisitely shaped. Altogether Rosamond Tracy was a beautiful woman.

"Had a good time this afternoon, Rosamond?"

"A good time? Oh, well enough. Garden parties are always stupid things," she answered, slowly.

He saw that she was out of sorts.

"Your uncle's ward has come out wonderfully this afternoon," she said presently, and not without a touch of bitterness. "She is quite the star of the afternoon. How deeply smitten Mr. Marcham is. Won't you find it rather difficult to accustom yourself to 'Aunt Dorothy'?"

"Oh, come now, don't be so absurd," said Fred, quickly. "That's all nonsense. Why, Uncle Roger is old enough to be her father."

"That's nothing, and it *will* be, you will see," she said, significantly. "Everyone is speaking of it, and really it will be a very good thing for her, as she has nothing of her own."

"Oh, that's stuff. Her father was very well off. She has plenty of means."

"I don't think so. At least Mr. Marcham told papa she had nothing. But that was in confidence. I suppose she doesn't know, and you needn't be so kind as to tell her."

"There isn't much confidence about it, now that your father and mother and you and I know," said Fred, coolly. "But I don't believe it all the same. I'll ask the girl."

"You'd better not," said Rosamond, quietly. "And if they are to be married, it does not matter."

"But they're not going to be married," said Fred, hotly. "I tell you the thing's absurd, and they've never thought of it for a moment."

"You are very confident, but if you marry

her it will be the same thing," said Rosamond, bitterly. "Then there won't be anybody to heir Underwood but yourselves."

"I mean to marry her, and they know it; at least Dorothy does," said Fred, tossing down his cigar and sliding off his perch. "As we don't seem to agree very well to-day, Miss Tracy, I think I'll go back to the lawn."

CHAPTER IV.

FRED'S REVENGE.

"YOUR ward is a charming young lady, Mr. Marcham," said Mrs. Tracy, in her sweetest tones. "I am sure she must make a great difference in Underwood."

"In what way, Mrs. Tracy?" asked the Squire, in that quiet way of his. To see him standing unconcernedly sipping his tea and looking so indifferent one would not have imagined the subject was in the least interesting to him. But the deep look in his eyes told a different tale as they turned to where Dorothy sat, the centre of an admiring group, with whom she was talking and laughing merrily, and looking lovely in her animation.

"Oh, come now, Mr. Marcham," said Mrs. Tracy, coquettishly. "Do you mean to say a pretty woman makes no difference in a house?"

"A woman of any kind makes quite a difference," he answered, with a slightly amused smile. "My ward is a very quiet young lady."

"Is she? Look at her now and hear her laugh," said Mrs. Tracy, nodding towards the group under the acacia tree. "No doubt she finds Underwood a little dull, poor girl."

"Has she said so, Mrs. Tracy? I am very sorry, but not surprised. It is dull for a young

40

girl," said Roger Marcham, and his face clouded
a little. "I have offered to get a companion
for her, but she will not hear of it."

"She will be all right now Mr. Wellesley has
come," she said, significantly. "I saw the
difference at once to-day when he was at her
side. Is the marriage to be soon? I have
heard so."

"I don't know if it is to take place at all. I
have not been told," said Roger Marcham,
coldly. "I am afraid Dame Rumour has taken
time too rudely by the forelock."

"Oh, how oddly you speak. Is the date not
really fixed? I am surprised, they seem so
utterly devoted to each other, and what an im-
provement she has made in Fred. Such a sad,
idle boy he was, wasn't he, Mr. Marcham? Miss
Vance is very proud of her work, Rosamond
says, and she has reason to be."

"Dorothy has made a friend of your daughter,
then, Mrs. Tracy?"

"Oh, yes; they are inseparable, and Rosamond, dear girl, cannot have one secret from
me, and I am glad of it. But I hope I am not
telling tales out of school, Mr. Marcham," said
Mrs. Tracy, with a little, affected smile. "Girls
always have their little secrets about their
lovers, you know."

"I suppose so," said Roger Marcham, absently.
It was as if a cloud had fallen across the
cheerful sunshine of that summer day. Yet
why should he care. He had long since told
himself he was old and gray, and that he could
only expect to be set aside, while others tasted
the sweets of life's young prime.

"What a stranger you have been at the Vicarage of late, Mr. Marcham," said Mrs. Tracy, presently.

"Have I? I am a busy man, and if my ward comes and goes, you know you are not forgotten at Underwood," he answered.

"Old friends are the dearest, as Rosamond said the other day, when we spoke of you never coming. She misses you from the Vicarage, Mr. Marcham."

"It is very kind of you to say so. It is pleasant to be missed," he answered; but his tone was neither eager nor interested. He was too honest and straightforward to understand the woman's hints, and too generous to suspect her of any plotting.

"Ah, there is Fred! See how he makes for the acacia tree!" laughed Mrs. Tracy. "It will be a good marriage for your ward, Mr. Marcham. You have not had a long term of office as guardian. Will they live at Underwood afterwards?"

Roger Marcham bit his lip. He was tried to the limits of his endurance.

"I really cannot speak definitely about matters which have never been presented to my mind, Mrs. Tracy," he said, courteously but coldly. "It is six o'clock. Would you think it very ungracious of me to leave now?"

"Leave? You have only come, but I see some of them moving. Mr. Marcham, could I trouble you to go through the shrubbery and find Rosamond? I saw her go there a little ago. She must say good-bye to the Maurices. Oh, thanks so much," she added, as he turned readily to grant her request.

Roger Marcham was not sorry to turn his

back on the gay party and be alone even for a moment. He felt amazed at, and impatient with, himself for being so cast down by the woman's talk. He knew it to be unfounded gossip, or, at the best, the merest supposition, and yet the possibility that it might contain a germ of truth made it intolerable to him. Poor Roger Marcham! the maiden from over the sea had indeed made havoc of his peace of mind. He met Rosamond Tracy at the gate leading into the paddock, and she looked surprised to see him.

"Mrs. Tracy has sent me to find you, Miss Rosamond," he said, cheerfully, trying to throw off the depression which weighed upon his spirits. "I think some of the guests are leaving."

"Oh, are they? I wonder what you will think of me, Mr. Marcham, if I say I am very glad? This has been an insufferably stupid afternoon, and I am glad it is over."

Roger Marcham smiled, but did not contradict her. Presumably he had found it so himself. They turned and walked together back to the lawn. Dorothy Vance saw them the moment they came through the shrubbery, and her eyes drooped. She had missed her guardian, and wondered why he had held aloof from her so persistently all afternoon.

"Mrs. Tracy has kindly excused me, Dorothy, and I am going off," he said, when he came to her side. "You and Fred need not hurry; there will be a full moon to guide you back."

"Oh, shall I not go now?" said Dorothy, almost eagerly, rising to her feet.

"No, no, my dear, stay and enjoy yourself

with the others. There is to be a dance by-and-by, and you know I would be of no use then," said Roger Marcham, kindly, but as he would have spoken to a child.

"Very well," she answered quietly, and turned her head away. She was hurt by his words, and fancied he was glad to be rid of her for a time. It was a curious thing how these two misunderstood each other continually, how their oversensitiveness magnified trifles, and their pride made barriers of reserve between them.

There was a pleasant dance for the young people on the lawn in the sweet summer dusk, but the charm of the day was gone for Dorothy Vance, and she was glad when they began to drop away one by one, and she could say to Fred they had better go home. Fred was more than ready, the prospect of the walk through the pleasant field paths with Dorothy as his companion was very bright, and he inwardly blessed his uncle for having the good sense to leave them to themselves.

"He'll ask her to-night," said Rosamond Tracy to herself, very bitterly, as she stood at the drawing-room window and watched the pair cross the little park. "I can't understand what there is about that little country girl to captivate both uncle and nephew. I wonder which she'll have?"

"Rather a nice affair, eh! Dorothy?" said Fred to his companion.

"What?" she asked with a start, for her thoughts were not with her companion. "The party? oh, yes, very nice."

"I don't believe you enjoyed it a bit. Don't

be in such a hurry. Let's go slow. It's not often I have the chance to walk or talk with you," said Fred, in rather a reproachful voice.

"It is getting dark, and see how wet the grass is. Mr. Marcham always warns me against the dews," she answered, without slackening her pace.

"Oh, of course, anything for him," said Fred, chewing the top of his stick, rather angrily. "Say, Dorothy, haven't I been working like a hatter, lately?"

"Like a what?"

"Oh, well, I beg your pardon; like a galley slave, then. Nine blessed hours every day I sit on that stool, and an uncommon hard stool it is, I can tell you."

"I am glad to hear it, but it is only your duty, Fred."

"Oh, well, that's poor enough encouragement for a fellow who finds duty an uncommon bore," said Fred. "I don't suppose you had the ghost of an idea what an effort it is for a fellow to be as conscientious as I have been all spring and summer."

"But are you not far happier?" asked the girl, and she lifted her sweet, earnest eyes to his face for a moment. That look made Fred's heart beat and his pulses tingle; he really cared for her, and had honestly endeavoured to do well for her sake.

"Oh, well, I suppose I am. If I thought you cared, or were glad, because I was really grinding, I'd be happier though," he said, eagerly.

"So I do care. Haven't I always scolded you since I came to Underwood?" she asked, and her laugh rang out sweet and clear in the still night air. "Of course it is delightful to think one's efforts are bearing fruit, and your uncle is very happy over it, Fred."

"Is he? I don't care a fig for that. The guv. and I never got on very well, Dorothy; he's so uncommon hard on a fellow."

Dorothy said nothing, but her lips shut together in a close, displeased manner, and her eyes flashed a little with indignation. Fred, however, not observing these ominous signs, went on.

"You see, he's always been such a proper model man all his days, he has no sympathy for a fellow who likes a little fun. He thinks a fellow should have Methuselah's head on his shoulders without his years, 'pon honour he does. He's just a trifle antiquated, the guv., though he thinks no end of himself."

"He has been the kindest of friends to you, Fred, and I will not listen when you speak so," said Dorothy, in a low voice. "We will change the subject, if you please."

"Wish you'd stick up for me as you stick up for the guv.," said Fred, ruefully. "I'll tell you what it is, Dorothy, I wish you'd never come to Underwood."

"Why?"

"Oh, just because you sit on a fellow so frightfully, when he's doing his best to please you. What do you suppose I went up to that old office to grind for if not to please you?"

"Well, I am pleased; but I wish you would work for your uncle's sake, and for the sake of working, because it will make you more like him," Dorothy answered candidly. She had not the slightest idea what Fred was aiming at, or she would not have spoken as she did.

"What an awful lot you think of the guv.," said Fred, a trifle savagely. "Look here, Dorothy, do you mean to have me or not? I like you such a jolly lot, I can't do without you."

"Have you?" The girl repeated the two words in a slow, bewildered fashion, and involuntarily stood still, and looked straight into her companion's face. They were now within the Underwood grounds, and had reached a quaint, little rustic bridge, which spanned the trout stream behind the house. The moon had risen—a glorious moon at its full—and the light was almost as clear as that of the day.

The girl's graceful figure in white, with its rich crimson wraps, stood out well against the shadow of the trees, her face somewhat pale, as if she were tired, was lighted by the radiance of the moon. Looking on that sweet face, Fred Wellesley thought it the loveliest and the dearest in the world. He was in earnest. Dorothy Vance had really touched his heart, and awakened in him some longings after a nobler, manlier life.

"I mean what I say, Dorothy; I love you; will you be my wife?" he repeated, this time yet more earnestly.

"Your wife? Oh, Fred, how can you think of such a thing?" she said, hurriedly, and her colour rose in a fitful wave. "Don't speak about it. It could never be."

"But I will speak about it. I'm in jolly earnest. I thought about it, I believe, the very night you came to Underwood. You are so dif-

ferent from other girls, a fellow couldn't help
caring about you. Do say you 'll have me some
time, Dorothy, and I 'll work indeed—do anything to please you, indeed I will."

As he spoke the girl's distress increased. He
was so evidently in earnest, and her answer
could only be an unalterable no.

"Oh, Fred, don't say any more; let us go in.
It can't be."

"Not just now, of course, nor for a long time.
I only want you to say it 'll be some day," he
pleaded, eagerly.

"But I can't say it. I would never care
enough for you to marry you. I must be plain,
nothing else will satisfy you. Let us go
home."

A look of bitter chagrin came into the young
man's face, and he struck the parapet of the
bridge an angry blow with his cane. He was a
hot-headed, impulsive, hastily-spoken youth, not
one who could accept a great disappointment
philosophically, or even calmly. And, in spite
of Rosamond Tracy's words, he had made very
sure of his uncle's ward.

"You don't know what you 're doing refusing
me, Dorothy," he said in the haste of anger.
"You have nothing. If Uncle Roger were to
marry, as no doubt he will, what will become of
you? You would need to go and earn your
own living."

She drew her slight figure up, her face paled,
her lips curled in scornful pride.

"I beg your pardon. I was independent
before I ever saw your uncle or Underwood,"
she said, sharply. "I need not make my home
here unless I choose. I cannot choose much

longer if I am to be treated as you have treated me."

"I tell you I'm right," said Fred, throwing prudence to the winds. "He told the Vicar your father left nothing; that you are dependent on him."

The girl's bosom heaved, her face grew paler, until her very lips were white.

"I don't believe it. I shall ask him to-night," she said, with difficulty; she had received a cruel blow.

"And if he marries Miss Tracy, as I believe he will," continued Fred recklessly, seeing the impression he had made, "what can you do? Come, Dorothy, let's be friends. I would be so good to you, for I *do* care a lot for you; and I didn't mean to hurt you, but what I said is true, you know it is. You can ask him if you like, he couldn't deny it."

But Dorothy did not hear the last words. She turned from him, and with a bursting sob fled up through the park towards the house. And yet, could she go in? If what Fred said were true, had she any corner in the world she could call her own?

CHAPTER V.

A WOUNDED HEART.

DOROTHY VANCE had been very happy at Underwood. She had accepted the sunshine which had fallen across her path without giving the future a thought, or even troubling herself about the often times troublesome question of ways and means. In her Indian home she had been accustomed to every comfort—her father, perhaps unwisely, had never permitted a shadow of his own care to rest upon his only child; had never hinted even that the day might come when she would be obliged to think out the question of mere livelihood for herself. He had left her in absolute faith to his friend, Roger Marcham, but it was not through Roger Marcham the trouble was to come on the child. She was a child in some things, though in others a proud, sensitive, high-souled woman. She was a child certainly in her knowledge of the world, evidenced by her entire belief in what was uttered by Fred Wellesley in a moment of passion. She was so absolutely truthful herself in word, act, and thought that the idea of wilful untruthfulness in others did not readily present itself to her mind. As she sped on towards the house that night one thought was uppermost in her mind, that she was a burden on her guardian, a burden so keenly felt that he had complained of it to others.

It was a cruel thought. Her cheeks tingled, her eyes filled with bitter, rebellious tears; it was so hard to think that she had remained so long trespassing on an unwilling kindness, only because she was in ignorance of the real state of the case. It was not kind, she said to herself, that Roger Marcham should have extended a half-hearted welcome, should have allowed her to humiliate herself as she had done, accepting his charity as if it were her absolute right. If she had ever given the matter a thought, she had fancied that her father had left ample means that her residence at Underwood was simply a matter of duty and inclination. She had been left Roger Marcham's ward, and had supposed it the right thing to reside under her guardian's roof. In the first misery and humiliation of her pain, Dorothy Vance was not just to Roger Marcham. It was a curious thing how swift she was to forget all his goodness, his unnumbered acts of courtesy and generous consideration; or, if they were remembered, they were so distorted as to appear like injuries which stabbed her to the heart. Every word or act which by any possibility could be construed into proof of Fred's assertion rose up before the girl's tortured imagination with painful vividness. Before she had reached the house she had convinced herself that she was an intruder, endured rather than welcomed under her guardian's roof. Her sensitive soul writhed under the sting of the obligation which seemed to weigh her down. For nine months she had eaten the bread of

charity as if it had been her own by right. Poor
Dorothy Vance! It was as if every bright
memory, every happy and beautiful thing in life,
had disappeared for ever, leaving only the dark
shadows of despair on her heart. The hall door
stood wide open, that hospitable door she had
loved and looked upon as the entrance to her
home. She sped through it with hurried foot-
steps, like a hunted thing who had no right
there. The library door was a little ajar, and at
the side of the velvet curtains which hung outside of it a gleam of yellow light indicated that
the master was within. As she sped past it, she
heard him stirring in the room, and presently a
footfall cross the floor. She had reached the
drawing-room landing, however, before the cur-
tain was swayed aside and Roger Marcham
looked out into the hall. She did not know
what made her pause and look over the
balustrade; perhaps the thought occurred to
her that she might not look upon his face again
for long. She admitted to herself, with a pang
of self-scorn, as her eyes dwelt for a moment on
the grave, somewhat careworn, features, that it
was the face she loved best on earth. She
did not know with what manner of love her
heart was filled, whether she regarded Roger
Marcham with the feelings a ward might enter-
tain for a guardian, who was supposed to fill
the place of a father, but the love was there,
and it made the sting of her humiliation and
pain a thousand times harder to bear. As
she stood, Fred Wellesley came hastily into
the hall.

"All alone, Fred! Where's Dorothy?" she
heard Roger Marcham say, but the eagerness

with which he asked the question was quite lost upon her.

"We fell out on the way, and she ran off and left me," Fred answered, curtly.

"You ought not to have allowed that. Were you within the grounds when she left you?"

"Oh, yes, just at the bridge. She can't be many minutes upstairs," Fred answered with a short laugh, as he hung his hat on the rack.

Dorothy wished to hear no more, but hurried on to her own room, and locked the door from within.

"What did you fall out about to-night?" asked Roger Marcham, as his nephew followed him into the library. "I thought you were the best of friends."

"Oh, so we are; but we have our tiffs. She's so jolly hard on a fellow," said Fred, with unblushing coolness. "How did you like the affair to-day?—not badly managed at all, was it? Mrs. Tracy is really a clever woman. She can make a great deal out of nothing."

"She is certainly a successful entertainer," returned Roger Marcham, absently; and then conversation flagged between them. An hour passed, and there was no sign of Dorothy's appearance downstairs. At half-past nine the supper tray was brought into the library as usual. The inmates of Underwood lived quietly, and without ostentation, their meals were very simple, and did not entail much labour on the servants.

"Go upstairs, Martha, and see whether Miss Vance will come down," the master said to the girl who entered the room.

"Yes, sir," she answered, and ran upstairs at

once, but her knock at Miss Vance's door brought
no response.

"What's the matter; what are you knocking
there for?" asked the housekeeper, who happened to come downstairs at the moment.

"It's for Miss Vance. Supper's in, and the
Squire's been asking for her, Mrs. Maple."

"Oh, well, run down, and I'll see. I daresay
Miss Vance is tired with the long afternoon,"
said the housekeeper, as she tapped with her
own hand at the young lady's door.

"The supper's in, Miss Dorothy, and the
gentlemen are waiting. Are you not well, my
dear?" she asked, when she received no reply.

After a moment she heard a movement in the
room, and the door was unlocked.

"I was lying down, Maple," Dorothy
answered, in a low voice, and holding the door
only a little ajar. "Say to Mr. Marcham I have
a bad headache, and will not come down to-
night."

"I am sorry to hear that, deary. Let me get
you a cup of tea," said Maple, kindly, for the
young lady quite rivalled the Squire in her affections now.

"Oh, no, thank you; I couldn't drink it—
indeed I couldn't. Thank you quite the same."

"Well, let me come and bathe your head,
Miss Dorothy. I can't bear to leave you, and
the master wouldn't like it."

"Oh, he wouldn't mind," she answered,
quickly. "Just leave me, dear Maple. I am
going to lie down again; I'll be all right in the
morning."

"Well, if you must have it, miss, I suppose I
must go. Good-night, deary; try and get a good

sleep," said Maple, kindly, as she reluctantly went away, little dreaming that she had heard and seen the last of the Squire's ward for many a day.

Fred Wellesley seemed to be in good spirits that night. He talked incessantly, but his uncle gave him only divided attention, and went off early to bed.

"I'm going up to town by the early train," said Fred, as his uncle left, "so I'll say good-bye as well as good-night."

"The early train!" said Roger Marcham, with a smile. "That will be an unprecedented feat. Do you think you'll manage it?"

"Of course I will. Maple knows. She's to have breakfast for me at half-past six."

"Very well, my boy; I shall be the last to put anything in the way of your industry. It is a great satisfaction to me to see you working so well," said Roger Marcham, kindly.

Fred looked rather abashed. He was conscious that he scarcely deserved these kind words. In his talk with Dorothy Vance he had scarcely been loyal to his uncle, who had ever been his kind and generous friend.

"Oh, don't say anything. I'm a good-for-nothing fellow," said he, hastily, speaking the truth this time at least. "You'll be up soon in town, I suppose?"

"Next week. I have promised Dorothy a week in town before the season closes, so we shall be seeing a good deal of you. You deserve a holiday this year, Fred. Good-night. Don't over-sleep yourself, or the joke will be against you."

So they parted for the night.

It was the month of June, when the days were
a dream of loveliness and light, the nights laden
with the odours of the sweet summer-time, the
whole earth blessed with the fulness and the
promise of a coming harvest time. How lovely
were the early mornings at Underwood! Often
had Dorothy stolen out of doors before the household were astir, to enjoy the delicious freshness
of the young day. Many a time she had watched
the daisies opening under the sun's kiss, and seen
the dew-drops glittering in his beams. These
early walks had been delightful experiences for
her, and had given a healthful stimulus to her
whole being. On the morning after the Vicarage
garden party, she was astir almost as early as the
dawn. The light was breaking greyly into her
room as she moved very softly about, gathering
a few things together with a curious nervous haste,
which indicated a spirit excited and over-wrought.
Her face was deadly pale, her eyes encircled with
dark rings, her mouth set in a sad but resolute
curve. She had lain down for an hour or two
on the bed, but had not slept. Her nerves
were quite unstrung. She had wrought herself
into a state of nervous excitement, which, sooner
or later, would wear her out. During these
painful hours, imagination had been busy; she
had brooded over her fancied wrongs until she
saw only one way of escape from them. She
must go away from Underwood—where, she did
not know or care, only she must go. Surely
some where there would be a corner for her,
something for her willing hands to do; so she
made her resolve, poor girl, without realising the
momentous risks to which she was exposing herself. Her ignorance of the great and evil world

misled her here, and she made her resolve without a misgiving or a fear. Anything, she told herself bitterly, would be preferable to eating the bread of charity under Roger Marcham's roof. When she rose, she changed her white dress for one of dark woollen stuff, put on the travelling hat and veil she had worn on board the *Indus*, and into a small hand-bag put a few things most necessary, or most precious to her. She had not very much money to set out seeking her fortune— four sovereigns and a few odd shillings were all her purse contained. When she was quite ready she opened the door softly, and looked out anxiously into the corridor. As she did so, the hall clock struck the half-hour after three. When its echo died away, there was not a sound in the house. She stole downstairs softly, fearing lest the slightest creaking of the stair should alarm and waken any one in the house. In the entrance hall she paused a moment, irresolute. It would be impossible for her to turn the heavy lock of the great door without making a noise which would certainly betray her. In her perplexity she thought of the library windows which opened out upon the terrace. They would be bolted and barred, but the room was not in the vicinity of any sleeping chamber, it might be possible to open them unheard. She crept into the room, and noiselessly shut the door behind her. As she set her bag on the table, and looked at the papers and books there, at the chair pushed back, just as Roger Marcham had risen from it, her mouth trembled. The temptation came upon her to lift his pen and write a word of farewell, but she restrained herself, and moving over to the window, swept back with nervous hand the heavy curtains which hung down before the shutters. The bolts creaked a little as she removed them, and her heart beat with apprehension. With the haste of fear she unfastened both shutter and window, and threw open one side of the folding door, admitting a glorious flood of sunshine into the room. It was sunrise, and the exquisite radiance dazzled her hot, tired eyes. She caught up her bag, cast a lingering look round the familiar room where so many happy hours had been spent, and with a catching sob stepped out on to the terrace. As she did so, a little bird on a neighbouring bough suddenly burst into song, pouring forth a flood of melody, which, in spite of its very joyousness, brought the tears to Dorothy's eyes. Every living thing was rejoicing except herself.

How fair the summer morning, how indescribable, and how lovely the tints with which the sunrise had adorned the sky, how fresh and sweet the zephyrs, how full of light and beauty that exquisite dawn! But Dorothy saw none of it. Her eyes were full, and when at the turn in the avenue she looked back for the last time at the place she had learned to love as a dear and happy home, she saw it dimly through a mist of blinding tears.

CHAPTER VI.

GONE.

"ERCY me, the house 's been broken into."
Such was the exclamation the housemaid uttered when she entered the
library shortly after six o'clock that
morning. Dorothy, in the haste of her flight,
had left the window wide open, without giving
a thought to the consternation the appearance
of the room might give the maid when she came
in to do her work. She looked fearfully round
the room, almost expecting to behold a burglar
in some corner, and then fled to the housekeeper's parlour, where that good lady was
drinking a cup of tea, after having given Fred
Wellesley his breakfast. He had just left the
house in good time to walk to the railway
station. It was not so much the desire to
return to work which had caused him to make
such an unusal effort, as the reluctance to meet
his uncle's ward. He was already ashamed of
what he had said, and had an honest intention
of writing a letter of apology to Dorothy when
he got back to town.

Fred was not a bad-hearted fellow, only
weak and foolish, and much given to doing
and saying things without thought. But
his idle words this time were destined to

bear graver fruits than any he had yet uttered.

He did not brood long over adverse circumstances, but went whistling through the fields that morning feeling as jolly as possible, and wondering at finding early rising so delightful after he was really out of doors.

"Mercy me! Mrs. Maple, if the house hasn't been broken into!" repeated Martha, as she burst into the housekeeper's room.

"Nonsense, girl; how could it?" inquired Mrs. Maple, without much appearance of concern.

"It is, I tell you; come to the library an' see. *You* haven't been in the library, have you, or Mr. Fred?"

"No, I haven't, and I know he hasn't, because he came straight here and had his breakfast, and I went myself with him to the door," returned Maple, rising from her chair. "What's happened in the library?"

"The windows is wide to the wall, that's all. It gave me quite a turn."

"That's queer," said Maple. "The master isn't up either. Are you sure you bolted 'em last night — you're rather careless, you know, Martha?" she added, severely.

"I didn't, but I stood by while the Squire did it, when I went in to light the candles," answered Martha. "Come down and see."

Now rather alarmed, Maple followed Martha downstairs, as fast as her portly figure would allow her, and together they entered the library. Maple went straight to the window and examined the bolts, with some satisfaction to herself.

"There ain't no burglars in it, girl. Whoever's opened them bolts has opened 'em from the inside. But who's done it?"

Martha shook her head.

"If they'd been burglars, Martha, them silver candlesticks would ha' been gone, an' the inkstand, an' dear knows what else," said Maple, looking perplexedly round.

Just then her eye fell on something lying just inside the window, and she stooped and picked it up. It was a girl's tan glove, with six pearl buttons at the wrist.

"What do you suppose is the meanin' o' this, Martha? That's Miss Dorothy's glove?" she asked, with a broad smile.

"Maybe she's out for one of her walks, an' left the window open," suggested Martha, smiling too.

"Of course, and you're a silly fool to come troubling a person with your nonsense. The house broke into, indeed! Not while I'm in it," said Maple, and marched off in high dudgeon.

Eight o'clock was the breakfast hour at Underwood. Roger Marcham was surprised to find himself first in the dining-room that morning; he was accustomed to find his ward in her place every morning when he came downstairs. He waited for some time, and even strolled out to the terrace to see if she was about the grounds, and so half an hour passed. This was such an unusual occurence, that, meeting the housemaid in the hall as he went in, he asked her to go up and ask whether Miss Vance was quite well.

"Oh, sir, I think Miss Vance is out; at least, the library window was open very early," she returned, smiling at the remembrance of her alarm, "and she had dropped her glove on the way out. Mrs. Maple found it on the sill."

"It is unusual for Miss Vance to be so late, she is usually so punctual," said the Squire. "Run up, Martha, and see whether she has not come back."

"Very well, sir," returned Martha, and hastened up to Miss Vance's room. She was not surprised to find the door half open, but when she ventured in she stared in amazement. The bed was untouched, the white coverlet was straight and unruffled, as Dorothy had carefully smoothed it when she rose.

It was Martha's work to make the beds while the dining-room breakfast was going on. Little wonder, then, that she stood amazed.

"Well, I never!" she exclaimed, and ran to Mrs. Maple again to seek an explanation.

"You haven't been in Miss Dorothy's room, have you, Maple? This is the queerest mornin'! I wish you'd come and look, for I don't think she's slept in her bed, and the master's asking for her. It's nearly nine o'clock."

"Goodness, girl, you'll have an end o' me wi' your scares," said Mrs. Maple, in an aggrieved voice. Nevertheless she quickly followed Martha to the room, and regarded it with genuine alarm.

"No, it hasn't been slept in," she said. "What on earth is the meanin' o' this? I must go and speak to the master myself."

So saying, Maple made haste, much flurried, to the dining-room, where the Squire was waiting with some impatience for his breakfast.

"Ah, Maple, good morning. Is Miss Dorothy well enough? She is very late."

"Well enough, sir? dear only knows. She ain't in the house, an' Martha an' me's just been up to her room, sir, an' she hasn't been in it all night; leastways she's not been in bed."

"What?"

"It's true, sir. I never got such a turn. Did Martha tell you about the library windows being open at six o'clock this morning?"

"She said something about it, and about a glove being found. Was that before Mr. Fred went away?"

"No, sir; immediately after. I had just seen him out o' the door, an' was sittin' down to a cup o' tea, when Martha comes runnin' up like a scared thing, saying there was burglars in the house. When I goes down, sir, the windows is open sure enough, but they was open from the inside, an' there's the glove I picked up. It's Miss Dorothy's, sir. She had 'em on yesterday with her white frock, which is lyin' all crumpled up on the floor."

During her speech, Maple had brought herself up to a pitch of excitement which found relief in tears. Roger Marcham took the dainty glove from her hand, crushed it in his own, and with set, stern face strode upstairs to see for himself the room they said his ward had deserted. It was just as Maple had described it, and a fearful anxiety laid hold upon the man's heart. He was not only anxious, he was completely astounded, for in all his imagination he could find no explanation for this extraordinary freak of his ward.

That was a strange morning at Underwood. Every corner in the house was searched, and the grounds explored also, but without avail. Then a messenger was sent over to the Vicarage to ask a question which set the inmates in a flutter of excitement. It was a strange thing to be asked, whether Miss Vance had spent the night at the Vicarage, but when Mrs. Tracy tried to get some information out of the groom, she met with no success. He had been enjoined by his master not to wait, nor answer any questions, but only to find out whether anything was known about Miss Dorothy there, and ride back at once. When the man brought word that they had seen or heard nothing of her since she left the Vicarage with Fred Wellesley at half-past eight on the previous night, Roger Marcham himself mounted his horse and rode off to the railway station at Morton.

"Good morning, Cunliffe," he said to the station-master, who ran out to learn the Squire's business. "Had you many passengers by the early train this morning?"

"Not a soul except Mr. Wellesley, an' I could hardly believe my eyes when I saw him come whistling into the station at six forty-five," said the station-master with a smile.

"You are quite sure no lady took ticket here?"

"Quite sure, sir, for I was on the platform all the time, but I'll ask the clerk," returned Cunliffe, in some surprise; and went off to the office at once.

In a few moments he came back, shaking his head.

"Nobody but Mr. Fred took a ticket this morning, sir. Pardon me, but you look worried. Is it any trouble, sir?"

"Trouble? Yes. I am in torture, Cunliffe. The most extraordinary thing has happened. My ward, Miss Vance, has disappeared from Underwood; and I came down, hoping she had only gone up to town for the day with my nephew," said the Squire, unable to hide his alarm.

"Oh, sir, she may have gone to see some friends, maybe down to Midgate," said Cunliffe, reassuringly. "Did she not say anything like that?"

"No, but you are right. It is quite possible she may have gone to Midgate," said the Squire, giving his impatient horse the rein. "Say nothing about it in the meantime, Cunliffe."

"All right, sir; good morning," said the station-master, with a respectful touch of his cap. As the Squire rode out of the station gate he met Mr. Tracy, who looked anxious and uneasy.

"What's this I hear, Mr. Marcham?" he said, stopping straight before the Squire's impatient horse. "What has happened at the Hall? Is anything wrong with Miss Vance?"

"I cannot tell, Mr. Tracy. She has left us; why or wherefore I cannot tell," said Roger Marcham, wearily. "I wish I knew what it meant. She must have gone either in the night or very early this morning, but what could be her object? You saw her more lately than I. Did she not seem in good spirits when she left the Vicarage?"

"In excellent spirits; in fact she was the life of the party," said the Vicar. "You can think of nothing which could make her leave?"

"Nothing. She seemed happy and at home with me. She said sometimes she was," said Roger Marcham, hopelessly. "I cannot understand it, and I am quite at a loss what to do."

E

"If you find no clue you had better go up to London and see your nephew. He was in conversation with her last you say?"

"He was. I'm riding round to Midgate to see whether she was observed at the railway station there this morning. If London was her destination (though I cannot for the life of me imagine why she should go there) she would naturally avoid Norton, knowing Fred was going from here this morning. They had some words last night on the way home, he told me. I wonder if that could have anything to do with it? Do you think they are attached to each other?"

"Miss Vance cares nothing at all for your nephew. I believe I am right in saying her whole affection is given to you," said the Vicar, warmly, for he saw that his friend was in sore need of some comfort. Roger Marcham shook his head.

"Then why should she leave me? I must go on, Tracy. I cannot stand this frightful suspense. Pray that this strange mystery may be cleared up."

"I will. God bless you!" was the Vicar's fervent response, and then Roger Marcham rode off at a gallop. In his state of mind inaction was misery. His inquiries at Midgate proved of no avail. It was market day in the town, and the early trains had brought a large number of country folk in, rendering the station so busy, that the arrival or departure of one individual could not have been noticed. Roger Marcham put up his horse at the Station Hotel, and, telegraphing his intention to Underwood, took the noon train for London. Before two o'clock he was in the office in Mincing Lane.

He found Fred Wellesley at his desk as usual, and evidently bent upon his work.

"Hulloa! Uncle Roger!" he exclaimed, in amazement. "What brings you here in such a hurry?"

"Come into my room, Fred," was his uncle's brief response, and Fred followed, with a vague feeling that something serious had brought him to town.

"Do you know anything about Dorothy, Fred?" was the first unexpected question, asked the moment the door was shut upon them.

"Dorothy! What about her?" exclaimed Fred. "Has anything happened to her?"

"Heaven only knows! She has gone away from Underwood, and we can find no trace of her anywhere."

The ruddy colour died out of the lad's face, and his hand shook. Conscience-stricken, he dared not look into his uncle's face.

"She did not sleep in the house last night," continued Roger Marcham, "and the maids found the library windows open at six o'clock this morning. I came up to ask about the quarrel you had last night. What was it about? and did you part in anger? In the first place, is there any understanding between you?"

"No; but I'll tell you all I know. I asked her last night to marry me, and she refused," said Fred, in a low voice.

"Yes, and what more? How did she leave you?"

"I must tell you the whole of this miserable business, Uncle Roger," cried Fred, in real distress. "I got mad when she said she didn't care about me, and I said if she didn't have me she'd lose a good chance, or something like that, because she was dependent on you, and if you married she would have no home."

"By what right did you make any such statement in my name?" asked Roger, in a cold, stern voice, his face white with righteous anger.

"I don't know. Rosamond Tracy told me all that, and I didn't care last night what I said," said Fred, in a low voice.

"And how did she receive your information?" asked Roger Marcham, in a choking voice.

"She said it wasn't true, that she'd ask you. She seemed to feel it awfully, for I believe she cares no end for you," said Fred, taking a curious delight in telling the worst. "She ran off to the house, and I never saw her again."

"May God forgive you, boy, for your cruel thoughtlessness," said Roger Marcham, hoarsely, and great beads of perspiration stood on his brow. "I tremble to think what a sensitive, high-souled girl such as Dorothy might be tempted to do in such circumstances. Pray that the consequences of your wicked folly may not be more than you or I can bear."

CHAPTER VII.

A SAFE HAVEN.

DOROTHY VANCE was not likely ever to forget the walk she took through field and meadow that June morning. As she walked leisurely along the narrow paths, brushing the dew drops from the wild-flowers with her skirts as she passed, she was keenly alive, even in the midst of her perplexity and care, to the extreme beauty surrounding her. It was one of the finest of summer mornings. The sun, early astir, poured a perfect flood of warm, golden radiance on the waking earth, every blossom opened its smiling eyes, every bird and bee made melody among flowers and trees; it was a happy dawn. Dorothy had her watch with her, and a pocket time-table, which she consulted sitting on a stile which separated the lands of Underwood from those of the Earl of Midgate. From it she learned that the train leaving Norton at 6.50 was due at Midgate at 7.15. She had ample time to reach the town before then, but the question arose, would Fred see her? The station would probably be quiet so early in the morning, the chances were that she could scarcely move along the platform and take her seat without being seen. If she were once in the train, she knew all would be right, for at Euston there would be no fear of meeting Fred. In a throng her safety lay. She pondered the thing sitting on the stile, with her little bag hanging on the gatepost, and her hat lying in her lap. She was hot and tired, the fresh morning zephyr was grateful to her weary eyes. She roused herself presently with an effort; eyes and heart had travelled, in spite of herself, over the fields to Underwood. She could see the square tower in the far distance, standing above the fresh green of the tree-tops. Somehow she felt less bitter against Roger Marcham this morning. She remembered more of his goodness and generous kindness. She was more just than she had been in the first agony of her wounded pride. She was thinking of him when the bell in Norton steeple rang five. If she intended to catch the early train at Midgate, she had no time to lose, for she had still seven good miles to walk. She dragged her tired limbs from the stile, tied on her hat, listlessly lifted her bag, and trudged on. She was bound for London; but what to do there, or where to go in the great city, was a question she had not yet faced. The first object was to get away from Underwood, to put miles between Roger Marcham and herself.

She kept to bye-paths and unfrequented roads, of which there were plenty in that neighbourhood, and avoided all chance of being seen. From the moment she quitted the Hall until she entered the streets of Midgate she did not encounter a living soul. The market town, however, was very busy, the square where the market was held already presented an animated appearance. The farmers' carts were all in, and the farmers' sons and daughters arranging their dairy produce on their stalls. The air was laden with the perfume of flowers and fruit and the baskets of strawberries among their cool green leaves. Dorothy bought one and a few biscuits before she went into the station, which she was glad to reach, and lie down for a few minutes on the hard sofa in the waiting-room. She had hurried very much during the last part of her journey, and arrived half-an-hour before the train was due. But she was completely worn out, and the moment her head touched the pillow she was fast asleep. The violent ringing of the bell and the hubbub of an arriving train aroused her, and she had only time to rush for a ticket, and jump into the train just as it started. Fred Wellesley was hanging out of the window of his compartment, but did not observe the slight figure step hastily through the crowd and disappear into a carriage.

Within the hour the train puffed into Euston, and Dorothy had reached the first stage of her destination. But what next? She had a vague idea that it would be possible for her to earn a living as a governess. She was an accomplished musician, but she little dreamed, poor girl, of the hundreds quite as capable seeking in vain for similar occupation in London. She emerged from the station, and going into the first restaurant ordered breakfast, for she was faint from want of food. The warm food refreshed her and gave her a new courage. The woman who served her, an elderly person with a kind face and pleasant manner, looked at her curiously as she took out her purse to pay. She was a lady it was easy to see. Perhaps it was natural for the woman to wonder what she was doing there alone.

"It's a fine morning, miss," she said, pleasantly, as she went with her to the door. "You'll enjoy a walk this morning, it's so sunny and clear."

"Yes, but I am tired. I am a stranger in London," she said, impelled to ask a word of help from the woman. "Perhaps you can tell me where I can find the nearest agency or register where I can inquire for a situation?"

"What kind of a situation, miss?"

"As a governess or music teacher."

The woman shook her head.

"Don't do that, miss. There's too many of them. You'd be better as a nurse in some nice family, but I don't think you are used to work."

"I have certainly led a very idle life hitherto," the girl answered, with a faint smile. "But I must work now."

"Friends dead?"

"Yes, all dead."

"Ah, that's bad. Do you know anybody in London?"

"Not a creature."

"That's worse. You are too pretty and too young to go about here alone. There's an agency at Bell's Causeway, two streets off. You might go there and inquire. And if you don't mind comin' back, I'll let you have a bit o' dinner cheap. I can't bear to see young people like you wanderin' about lookin' for work. I'd like to hear how you get on."

"Thank you," said Dorothy, lifting pathetic, grateful eyes to the woman's face. "I shall be sure to come back: and as to the dinner," she

added, with a faint smile, "I can pay the usual
sum for it. I have a little money, which I hope
will last me till I get something to do."

Her new friend shook her head and went back
into the shop with a troubled look on her face.
She was a country woman, not yet hardened into
city ways; her heart was large and hospitable.
Perhaps that was the reason why, though her
restaurant was popular, she made so little profit.
She erred in generosity rather than in meanness
towards her customers. But she was happy and
contented, and so long as she managed to make
both ends meet did not trouble herself about
large profits. Dorothy Vance was not the first
friendless girl she had helped forward in the
struggle for existence.

Dorothy had left her bag at the restaurant,
and though she was eager to find something to
do, somehow she seemed to lack energy even to
go in search of it. She was worn out in body
and mind, and her heart had gone back with
painful longing to the dear home she had left.
A wish began to form in her mind, a regret
that she had not been fair and open with Roger
Marcham, and asked for confirmation or denial
from his own lips. Even for the kindness he had
shown, she told herself he was entitled to that.
She went out of her way in her preoccupied
mood, and it took her nearly an hour to reach
the office, though she might have walked the
distance in twenty minutes. When she entered
the place, a very pert, but business-like young
woman, rather patronisingly asked what she
wanted.

"A governess's place? Oh, yes, we have
several on our books. Half-a-crown, please, to

enter your name as an applicant, and then I'll give you the addresses, then half-a-crown when you are suited. These are our terms, and they are very moderate, considering that our business is with the best families. What are your qualifications, miss?"

"I am afraid I cannot say proficient in anything except music and drawing," said Dorothy, faintly. "May I sit down, please? I am very tired."

"Oh, certainly sit down. Well, here is one, I think, which might suit," said the young woman, running her finger down a long list of names in the ledger. "Mrs. St. Clair Goodwin, 14 Elmira Villas, Clapham. She laid special stress on the music, I remember. There are five children, and the salary is fourteen pounds."

"Fourteen pounds? Surely that is very little. Our housemaid——" began Dorothy, and quickly checked herself. But the young woman looked at her with curious suspicion.

"When you have no languages you won't get any more," she said, severely, yet with a kind of easy familiarity which somehow annoyed Dorothy. "Well, will you take the address? But I may tell you Mrs. St. Clair Goodwin will be very particular about references. She is one of our most fastidious customers."

"Clapham—is that far?" Dorothy asked, ignoring the insinuation contained in the woman's speech.

"A good bit. You will get the underground train in the next street. What is your name, please?"

"Dora Verney," replied Dorothy, but her colour rose, and she hastily drew down her veil.

" All right—Miss Dora Verney. Will you go out to Mrs. St. Clair Goodwin's just now ? "

" Yes, if I can get a train."

" Oh, there are trains every five minutes. You 'll let me know if you are suited. Your address, please ? "

" Oh, I have no address. I have just come from the country to-day."

" But you must be staying somewhere. I must have an address, miss."

" Well, twenty-three Gisborne Street." said Dorothy, giving the number of the place where she had breakfasted. " Good-morning."

So saying, she walked out of the office, with cheeks burning, and a curiously humiliated feeling in her heart. She had not thought there would be so many unpleasant things connected with the search for work. Poor Dorothy, she had scarcely tasted the bitterness of that thankless task, as she proved an hour later, when she was being interviewed by Mrs. St. Clair Goodwin in the drawing-room of many colours at number fourteen Elmira Villas. The lady anxious to secure the services of an accomplished governess for the sum of fourteen pounds was a large, pale, over-dressed woman, with a patronising style and a languid mode of speech, which seemed to indicate a kind of tolerant contempt for the whole world, and for governesses in particular.

" Oh, you are a person from the register," she said, when the slight, pale, young creature was ushered into her presence. " Well, what are your qualifications for the post you are seeking?"

" I believe I am a good musician. I have had the best of teachers," said Dorothy, falteringly, for her courage and hope were now at the lowest ebb. "I have had a good English education, and I would do my best, madam, if you would engage me."

"It requires consideration. I am afraid you are too young and inexperienced to maintain the discipline I like. My children are very high-spirited, especially Adeline, the eldest, a beautiful girl, Miss—Miss Verney, and possessing exceptional talents. She is with Saldini for music. You would require to superintend her practice, and teach her all other branches, while you would, of course, have the entire charge of the other four. All the governesses I have had have had the care of their wardrobes. I hope you are a good needlewoman, and can shape garments for children."

"Is that a governess's usual work, madam?" Dorothy felt impelled to ask.

There was nothing impertinent in the question, but it seemed to displease Mrs. St. Clair Goodwin.

"I left all particulars with the person at the office, just to save myself the needless answering of questions," she said, stiffly. "If you are not prepared to undertake the work you may go, Miss Verney. There are hundreds who will gladly accept a home in a refined Christian family such as this."

"I beg your pardon if I have offended you. I only wish to know all that would be expected, and whether I could undertake it conscientiously," Dorothy forced herself to say, seeing she was losing ground. "What ages are the children?"

"Adeline is twelve, Leonard, the youngest, is

five," answered Mrs. Goodwin, somewhat molli-
fied. "But what kind of references have you?
In what sort of a family have you been serving
before? I am very particular about the morals
of any person who comes in contact with my
children, and insist that my nurse shall be a
pious woman, and go regularly to the chapel.
I should require my governess to follow her example."

"I have never been a governess before," said
Dorothy, rising, for she felt that the interview
might come to an end.

"Oh, have you not? Are you in reduced circumstances? Of course you will have references
from a clergyman, or some other responsible
person?" said Mrs. Goodwin, with a distrustful
gleam in her hard eyes.

"I have no references. I am quite alone and
friendless. I suppose it will be difficult to find
any one to trust me," said Dorothy, with a slight
bitterness of tone, and drawing down her veil
to hide the tears which trembled on her eye-
lash.

"You are right. There must be something
questionable about a person who cannot find a
creature to recommend her," said Mrs. Goodwin,
righteously. "Good-morning, Miss Verney.
Take the advice of one who knows what duty is,
and who does it with all her might, and go back
to your friends. I shall go into town this morning, and reprimand the register people for having a person without references on their lists.
One has to be so careful in choosing a companion or instructress for young people, that every
precaution must be taken."

Dorothy's cheeks flamed with indignation, but

she did not trust herself to speak. When she got outside the immaculate gates of Mrs. St. Clair Goodwin's abode she gave way to a burst of weeping. Happily it was a quiet thoroughfare, and no one observed her emotion. It was afternoon before she found her way back to Gisborne Street. Strange that she should look upon that poor little place as a haven of refuge, because in it a womanly woman had uttered a word of sympathy and kindness.

"Come away, miss, I was gettin' anxious about you," said the good soul, who had been strangely drawn by the sweet face and winning way of the young girl. "Bless me, how done you look. Did you find it as tough a job as I said? Ay, ay, cry away, poor thing; it'll do ye good. Just come into my back place, and we'll have a talk over it and a cup of tea. This is my quiet time, afore folks come in seekin' their teas. There's folks as has had their teas reg'lar in the shop for ten year, an' wouldn't take it no place else. That's the kind of business I like— customers that's friends as well. Ay, ay, you do look tired."

Dorothy followed her kind friend into a snug little back room furnished in chintz, and with a little muslin curtained window looking out on a green strip of grass in the back yard. A cheerful little fire crackled in the grate, and the kettle was singing on the hob, on the mantel shelf were curious and quaint little ornaments such as you see in country cottages, and there were a few flowers in a tall glass jug on the little table, and the whole place was homely and comfortable in the extreme.

"Sit down on the sofa, my deary, and I'll get

the tea in no time," said the good soul, bustling about pleasantly. This was an opportunity just after her own heart. Dorothy sat down on the pretty chintz sofa, and laid her head down on the pillow. She felt at that moment that she would not have exchanged that humble room, made bright by the sunshine of that happy, helpful heart, for the palace of a king. She felt as if, after being tossed about on some tempestuous sea, she had anchored in a sure haven of peace and safety.

They had a long talk over their cosy cup of tea, and it came to pass that Dorothy Vance slept that night in the chintz-covered room, and not that night only, but many nights following.

In the great wilderness of London her feet had been guided, and she had found a home.

CHAPTER VIII.

A HAPPY ENDING.

THE year was drawing to a close. The trees were all brown and bare, the December frosts had nipped the leaves even in sheltered corners, and given a brighter tinge of red to the dogberry and the hollies. There was a prospect of fine skating at Norton, and of a jolly hard Christmas, when there could be enjoyment both without and within. So hard was the frost during Christmas week that the trout stream in the Underwood grounds was frozen over for the first time within its master's memory. It was a pretty picture down at the rustic bridge, from which the icicles hung in all sorts of fantastic shapes, to watch the filmy lacework of the hoar frost on the bare boughs, and among the leaves of the evergreens. The place even in winter had a beauty all its own. The path by the trout stream was a favourite walk with Roger Marcham. Many a pleasant hour he had spent there with basket and rod—in the long summer days, with his ward at his side. The place was filled with associations and memories of her, and for that reason was full of painful interest to him. He loved it, and yet to come there after the desolation had fallen on Underwood was to him a source of keenest pain. By the end of December, six months after Dorothy's disappearance, he was absolutely without hope of ever looking upon her face again. Perhaps that was natural, seeing that every means he had taken to discover a clue to her whereabouts or her fate had been absolutely without success. He had spared no expense, the best skill the metropolis could afford had been placed at his disposal, but in vain. The missing girl had been traced to London—that is, it was ascertained at Midgate that a person answering to the description had taken a third-class ticket for London at the booking-office at Midgate, and there all inquiry had come to an abrupt end. Nobody had seen her at Euston or any intervening station, and to seek for a quietly-dressed young woman in London was rather a hopeless task.

The strange and anxious trial which had come upon Roger Marcham had wrought in him a great change. Those who loved him were amazed and grieved that he should lay the thing so terribly to heart. It was in vain they assured him he had nothing with which to reproach himself; that he had been more than kind to the girl who had treated him with such a strange ingratitude. It was the nature of the man to lay blame to himself. He tortured his imagination with recalling what he was pleased to think the indifference and lack of sympathy with which he had treated her; things which existed solely in his imagination, and had not the remotest foundation in fact. Perhaps it was not surprising that a coolness had existed between Roger Marcham and his nephew since that unhappy day on which Dorothy Vance left

Underwood.   Altogether matters were in a
very unsatisfactory state when the year drew
to its close.

It was the day before Christmas, a fine, clear,
frosty morning, in which it was a perfect delight
to be alive and out of doors.   The ground rang
clear and crisp under the tread; the fine sharp
air was more exhilarating than a draught of wine;
the sky was blue and brilliant; it was a choice
winter day.   After his solitary breakfast, Roger
Marcham left the house, and, with the dogs at
his heels, strolled down to the old bridge.   His
face, worn with the anxiety and misery of the
past months, wore a far-off expression, which
had in it a touch of pain.   He was recalling last
Christmas, which had been so royally kept at
Underwood in honour of his ward.   How grace-
fully she had taken her place at his right hand
at the festivities, and how keenly she seemed to
enjoy her first Christmas on English soil!   He
could not endure the thought of the morrow,
the chime of the Christmas bells would be a
discord in his ears.   For where would the child
his dead friend had entrusted to his care be
spending her Christmas Day?   With such
questions as these did Roger Marcham torment
himself.   He followed the windings of the
stream, the dogs running on its frozen and
uneven surface, until it lost itself in the lake, on
which he had taught his ward to skate.   He did
not linger there, however—the memory of these
delightful mornings was not pleasant to him now
—but called to the dogs ranging through the
thickets, and turned his step towards the house.
He had not gone many yards when he caught
the flutter of a calico gown among the trees,

"After his solitary breakfast, Roger Marcham
left the house."

and presently Martha, the housemaid, came running breathless along the path by the riverside.

"Would you come up, sir? There is a person wishing to see you from London, and she is in a hurry. She wants to go back, she says, by the twelve train, and it's after ten now."

"She?—is it a lady, Martha?"

"Yes; at least a woman, sir; like a tradesman's wife, I think. Very nice and pleasant, but she seems to be excited about something."

"She did not tell you her business?"

"No, sir."

"Perhaps one of my London tenants. My agent tells me they are always threatening to come down and interview me about their grievances. The frost is very hard this morning, Martha."

"Yes, sir."

"The dogs are rather mystified over the ice here," he said, pointing to the frozen stream. "I'll cross the park straight then, as the person is in such a hurry," said the Squire, and strode over the frosted grass without the remotest prevision of what he was about to hear. It never occurred to him to connect the visit of the stranger in any way with his lost ward.

Martha had put the woman in the little breakfast parlour in which the Squire had chosen to have his meals since he had been again left alone. A bright fire was burning there, and when Roger Marcham entered it he saw the woman, a stout, motherly-looking person, sitting, warming her hands before the comfortable blaze.

She got up rather nervously when the door

opened, and dropped an old-fashioned curtsey to the grave, gentlemanly-looking man who entered. As she did so, however, she looked at him keenly, with a pair of very shrewd, though kindly, grey eyes.

"Mr. Marcham, sir?" she said, inquiringly. "It's Mr. Marcham I want to see."

"I am Mr. Marcham," answered the Squire, courteously. "Pray sit down, and tell me what I can do for you. It is a cold morning for such an early journey as you must have taken. You have come from London, I think."

"Yes, and it is cold, but I didn't mind it much. I don't mind it at all, now I've got here," said the woman, with a curious little nod of satisfaction; then she opened a very large black bag, and took from it an envelope, carefully wrapped in brown paper.

"Would you look at that, please, sir, and tell me if you know the writing, or anything about it. I don't, but if you do, perhaps it'll be all right."

In some amazement Roger Marcham took the envelope in his hand, but the moment his eye fell on what was written on it, he gave a great start. It was his own name and address, written in full by the hand of his ward.

"Where did you get this, woman?" he asked, hoarsely. "Do you know who wrote it?"

"Yes, I know. I'm right, I see," said the woman, beginning to smile. "The person who wrote that, bless her poor dear heart, is in my house. Could you sit down, sir, till I tell you all about it? Yes, she's alive an' well, at least middlin' well. I don't know a thing about anything, but I see you're gaspin' to know *that*."

said the good soul, with a familiarity which was
not at all offensive. " Will you give me time,
sir, to tell my story ? "

" I 'll try, since you have so far relieved my
mind. I do not know who you are, or how you
have been connected with her who wrote this,
but I shall never forget that you have given me
the first ray of light in this unhappy business.
Please go on."

The woman nodded to herself several times,
and, sitting down, clasped her hands on her
knee and began—

" It was in the summer, sir, the month o' June,
just at the time o' the great heat there was such
a speakin' about, that there came into my shop
—I keep a little eatin' house, sir, in Gisborne
Street, off Euston Square—early in the mornin'
afore nine, a bit slip of a young lady, carrying a
bag, and lookin' very hot, and tired, and white,
poor lamb, and asked for a cup of tea and some
bread and butter. I served her myself, 'cos my
gal had just left me, and a good riddance, and
the one that came for an hour or two in the day-
time was late; so I served her myself. She
drank up the tea, but ate nothing, and I couldn't
but look at her with pity, she was that young
an' sweet, an' seemed so sad. I went to the door
with her when she was goin', an' spoke a bit
word about the weather to her, an' she asked me
did I know any place where she could look after
a situation as a governess, or sich like. I told
her of a place, but I advised her not—there's so
many, sir, an' it 's such a poor, hopeless sort of
thing. I 've known o' more'n one who broke their
hearts in it. But she went away, promisin' to
come back an' tell me how she got on. I

thought of her all day, sir, she was such a pretty creatur', and seemed so sorrowful, an' when she told me her friends were all dead, my heart was sore for her. The day was well on afore she came back, an' I knowed the moment I set eyes on her how she 'd fared. I 've seen that kind o' hopeless look in too many young faces in London, which is jes' old Babylon over again, as I allus say. Well, she came in an' was very broken down an' tired like, an' she had tea with me, and after a bit talk she went to bed in my little room. I 'm very particular about strangers, sir, but I knowed she were the right sort, an' I seed there were some sore trouble vexin' her heart. She never told me anything about herself, except that her father an' mother died in India, an' I know'd she was a lady by her look an' ways, an' I couldn't ask her questions. But somehow, sir, I didn't feel as if I needed to know all about her, she had such a way with her, just like a child for faith an' trust, and I couldn't bear the idea of her goin' away again. She said she 'd stop till she 'd get a place, but after a bit we never spoke about her goin', so she stopped an' stopped, an' there she is still."

"May God bless you!" fell fervently from the lips of Roger Marcham.

The woman nodded and went on. "No doubt she was glad o' the place an' the shelter, though my place is a poor little corner, but she was o' the greatest use to me, sir, an' has always been. There was nothing the child wouldn't do, sir, though she was a lady born, an' I 've never been so well off, or my legs so saved since ever I had the shop; but there was one thing I never let her do, nor wouldn't—go into the shop to serve the

folks. I knew, though she was so willin', that it
wasn't the place for her, an' that's the only pint,
sir, on which her an' me didn't agree: We were
very happy together, sir, although we knew
nothing about each other till that day. I never
know'd a more willin' helpful creatur' in my
whole life. I got to be as fond o' her as if she'd
been my own, but I never asked, nor she never
told, nothin' about her past. 'It's all done with,'
she used to say, but I watched her a good bit,
an' I saw quite well that she carried a sore heart
often, and that something seemed to be troublin'
her. She got to have such an anxious look, sir,
and a bit droop to her lips, that it vexed me
more than I can tell to see it. But she never
spoke, nor I never asked, but one day I found
that envelope accidental, and I made bold to
keep it, and put it away out o' sight. I said to
myself, sir, that if anything came over her I had
somebody I could go to. But still I never
spoke, nor did she, an' so the summer wore
away, an' it came the darker days, an' then I
thought my darlin' gettin' very thin an' white.
Excuse me, sir, for callin' her my darlin', but
you see I had got to love her as if she were my
own. Still I never spoke, but kep' watchin' her,
an' I saw the droopin' lip, an' the wistful eyes,
an' the listless way o' goin' about, an' I said to
myself—my precious, that can't go on. I saw
as well as I'd been told, sir, that something,
whatever it was, was preyin' on her mind, an'
she says to me one day quite suddenly, jes' as if
the words had got out all of themselves—'I believe
I did wrong.' Then I looks up quietly an' I
says, says I, 'Dora, my lamb, if you think so,
I know you'll set to work to mend that wrong.'

"Then her colour rose up very red, an' her eyes got wet, an' she says, with a bit sad shake o' her pretty head, 'It is too late now, Aunt Judith, and I am very happy with you.'

"I says not another word, sir, but I thinks the thing over an' over in my mind, an' after a deal o' thinkin' I comes down here to see if I could do anything, not knowin' whether it wouldn't be a fool's errand. Do you know my Dora, Mr. Marcham, or can you tell me anything about her or her folks? Is there anybody you know of that's a-hungerin' to see her, as I see she's a-hungerin' to see somebody, in spite o' the bit o' pride, or whatever it is, that's in my darlin's heart."

And good Aunt Judith wiped away a sympathetic tear from her kindly eye.

"May God for ever bless and reward you," said Roger Marcham, grasping her two hands firm and fast in his own. "You have kept, and will restore to me, I trust, my greatest earthly treasure. But, come, at the risk of hurrying you away, we must go and get that train; we can settle upon the way."

So saying, Roger Marcham rang the bell, ordered a hasty refreshment for the stranger, and bade them bring the carriage to the door at once.

He was like a man who had obtained a new lease of life. The maid could not but wonder what had wrought the change. Within the hour they were seated in a private first-class compartment of the London train, and there Roger Marcham unfolded to the kind woman, the story of Dorothy's flight. He told her the story in its entirety. She had earned the right to his confidence, and he gave it gladly. She was a poor, uneducated woman, but she had a heart of gold, and had rendered to Roger Marcham a service which he could never forget, or think of lightly. Had she not saved his ward from untold temptations and hardships? He could have kissed the toilworn palm, in token of his gratitude and honour. Although it was early in the day when they reached Euston, a thick fog hung so low over the city that gas lamps were lighted in the streets, as well as in every shop and warehouse. Roger Marcham accompanied his new friend to Gisborne Street with a beating heart. He could scarcely realise that in a few minutes he should look upon the sweet face he had so missed from his home.

"Just follow me, sir; she'll be in the back room; we're never busy at this time," said Aunt Judith, in an excited whisper when they reached the door. Then she marched boldly in, and met Dorothy just at the door of the inner room. The little passage between the two places was in shadow, so that Roger Marcham was hidden.

"Back again so soon, Aunt Judith!" Dorothy said, and the sweet voice went to the heart of Roger Marcham like the most exquisite music.

"Yes, my deary, here I am; an' here's somebody with me, who, I think, wants to see you much more than I want to. Here he is," said Aunt Judith, tremblingly, and then fairly turned about, and, sitting down on a chair in the shop, began to cry.

Dorothy stood still with a half-frightened look, as the tall figure emerged from the shadows. Then a strange, low cry, rung through the room, the door was shut, and Aunt Judith heard no more.

*   *   *   *   *

"My guardian has forgiven me, Aunt Judith, and he wants to say, what I never can, what I never will attempt to say, that we shall never forget what you have done for me."

It was Dorothy who spoke, and though her voice was trembling, there was the light of a strange and exquisite joy on her face. She had her hands folded on Roger Marcham's arm, and his hand, firm, kind, and true, was clasped above them. The other he held out to Judith Rainsford, but for the moment he was not able to speak. They did indeed owe to that kind-hearted woman an unspeakable debt of gratitude.

"Oh, it's all right, it's all right, but you'll have your teas surely afore you go. I suppose you'll be a-goin' to-night?"

"Yes," said Roger Marcham, finding his voice at last. "And so are you!"

"Me! where to?"

"Underwood. You must come and look after 'your darlin',' you know, until she becomes mine altogether. We are going to be married, Aunt Judith, so we'll shut up shop, shall we, and go?"

"Oh, I couldn't, sir. It wouldn't be fair to them that's been my friends so long. To leave them without their teas, sir, would be so cruel."

"Never mind. We don't stir a foot without her, do we, Dorothy?"

"No, most certainly not."

"I don't think we shall fall out again, Aunt Judith. We've had too severe a lesson," said Roger Marcham, gravely, yet with a dawning smile, as he saw the light in his darling's eyes. "It all arose out of a foolish child's imagination. But I think it would be safer to have you to look after us."

Aunt Judith was persuaded, and for the first time for many years the shop in Gisborne Street was shut up, and the customers had to go elsewhere for their "teas."

And when she once tasted the luxury and comfort of Underwood, it was not difficult to persuade her still further, and now she is a pillar in the house of Underwood, and the dear true friend of Roger Marcham and his happy wife. It is seldom they speak of the unhappy mistake which embittered so many months of their lives. The happiness of the present has quite wiped out that past bitterness. It was a serious lesson to Fred Wellesley, who is now a steady business man, happy in the house where Rosamond Tracy is a model wife and mother. Next to his own wife, he considers the sweet mistress of Underwood the best woman in the world, and Roger Marcham thinks the same, but does not admit of any exception whatsoever. As to Dorothy herself, I suppose I need scarcely say that she is a thousand times happier as Roger Marcham's wife than she was as Roger Marcham's ward.

THE END.

BOOKS

FOR

GIFTS AND PRIZES

TO

YOUNG PEOPLE

SELECTED FROM

OLIPHANT, ANDERSON & FERRIER'S

CATALOGUE

30 St Mary Street
Edinburgh

21 Paternoster Square
London, E.C.

Comrades True.   By Ellinor Davenport Adams.   Extra crown 8vo, with six original Full-page Engravings   3s. 6d.

In His Steps: "What would Jesus do?" By Charles M. Sheldon. Demy 8vo, cloth extra, gilt edges, with Frontispiece   .   3s. 6d.

A Handful of Silver. By L. T. Meade, Author of "A Girl in Ten Thousand," &c. With Illustrations .   3s. 6d.

Tales of the Covenanters. By Robert Pollok. With Life of the Author by the Rev. Andrew Thomson, D.D. General View of the Character, Literature, Aims, and Attained Objects of the Covenanters by the Rev. George Gilfillan, and with Twelve Illustrations by Mr H. M. Brock. Large crown 8vo, art canvas binding   .   .   .   .   .   3s. 6d.

Richard Tregellas: A Memoir of his Adventures in the West Indies in the Year of Grace 1781. By D. Lawson Johnstone. Sixteen Full-page Illustrations   3s. 6d.

Jeanie Wilson, the Lily of Lammermoor. Fourth edition 2s. 6d.

In Glenoran. By M. B. Fife. Crown 8vo, cloth extra, Illustrated   .   2s. 6d.

Adèle's Love: The Story of a Faithful Little Heart. By Maude M. Butler. Crown 8vo, cloth extra, with Frontispiece 2s. 6d.

Kate and Jean. The History of Two Young and Independent Spinsters, narrated by their Landlady. By Jessie M. E. Saxby. Frontispiece   .   .   .   2s. 6d.

When Hyacinths Bloom.

By Ida Jackson. Cr. 8vo, cloth extra, with Illustrations by Ida Lovering 2s. 6d.

The Stronger Will. By Evelyn Everett-Green. Crown 8vo, cloth extra, with Seven Full-page Illustrations . 2s. 6d.

Falconer of Falconhurst. By Evelyn Everett-Green. Crown 8vo, cl. extra, with Full-page Illustrations . 2s. 6d.

The Doctor's Dozen. By Evelyn Everett-Green. Crown 8vo, cloth extra, with Illustrations 2s. 6d.

Miss Uraca. By Evelyn Everett-Green. Crown 8vo, cloth extra, with original illustrations by Ella Burgess . 2s. 6d.

Judith. By Evelyn Everett-Green. Crown 8vo, cloth extra, with Illustrations . . . 2s. 6d.

In the Heart of the Hills. A Tale of the Pacific Slope. By Hattie E. Colter. Crown 8vo, cloth extra, with Illustrations 2s. 6d.

A Girl in Ten Thousand. By L. T. Meade. Post 8vo, antique paper, art canvas. Decorated Title and Frontispiece 2s. 6d.

Nature's Story. By the Rev. H. Farquhar, B.D. Post 8vo, cloth neat, with many Illustrations . 2s. 6d.

Facts and Fancies about Flowers. By Margaret Moyes Black. Post 8vo, cloth neat, with 14 Illustrations by C. C. P. . . . . . 2s. 6d.

The Luck of the House. By Adeline Sergeant. Crown 8vo, cloth extra, with Frontispiece . 2s. 6d.

Molly. By A. C. Hertford. With Frontispiece   2s.

The Wooing of Christabel. By Mrs Elizabeth Neal 2s.

In Her Own Right. By Mrs. Elizabeth Neal .   2s.

Adah, the Jewish Maiden:
A Story of the Siege of Jerusalem. By Agnes M. Gray .   2s.

From East to West; Stories of the Pilgrim Fathers. By Sarah M. S. Clarke   2s.

The Wish and the Way. By Mrs Meldrum .   2s.

The Young Brahmin. By Auguste Glardon   2s.

Scenes and Sketches from English Church History. By Sarah M. S. Clarke .   2s.

Sister Constance. By K. M. Fitzgerald .   2s.

Sifted as Wheat. By Mrs Elizabeth Neal   . 2s.

Bush and Town: A Story of the Pacific Coast. By C. Kirby Peacock   . . 2s.

Swirlborough Manor. By Sarah Selina Hamer   2s.

The Musgrove Ranch: A Tale of the Southern Pacific. By T. M. Browne   . . . 2s.

Under the Live Oaks. By T. M. Browne   . 2s.

Her Day of Service. By Edward Garrett, Author of "By Still Waters" .   . . 2s.

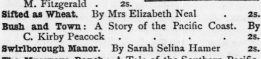

The Noble Printer: or, The Story of the First Printed Bible   2s.

The Duke's Ward. A Romance of Old Kent. By Dora M. Jones .   2s.

Carrageen and other Legends. By K. M. Loudon .   1s. 6d.

A Pair of Pickles. By Evelyn Everett-Green.   1s. 6d.

Little Miss Vixen. By Evelyn Everett-Green.   1s. 6d.

Puddin': An Edinburgh Story. By W. Grant Stevenson, A.R.S.A. With six Illustrations, and initial letters by the Author 1s. 6d.

Grizzly's Little Pard. By Elizabeth Maxwell Comfort. With three original Illustrations . 1s. 6d.

Private James Fyffe: A Story of the Boys' Brigade. By Herbert Reid. Illustrated . 1s. 6d.

Jacob Jennings, the Colonist: The Adventures of a Young Scotchman in South Africa 1s. 6d.

Peter the Great 1s. 6d.

Ned's Motto: or, Little by Little . 1s. 6d.

Crossing the Line: A Cruise in a Whaler . 1s. 6d.

Bertie Lee; or, The Threshold of Life 1s. 6d.

Ocean Venture: A Boy's Book of Sea Stories, Scenes, and Incidents 1s. 6d.

How the French took Algiers . . 1s. 6d.

Little Miss Conceit. By Ellinor Davenport Adams. With six original Illustrations and Decorated Title 1s. 6d.

Adolph, and how he found the "Beautiful Lady." By Fanny J. Taylor, with numerous Illustrations by Helene Toering 1s. 6d.

Jock Halliday: A Grassmarket Hero. By Robina F. Hardy . 1s. 6d.

Tom Telfer's Shadow. By Robina F. Hardy 1s. 6d.

Ben Hanson. By J. M. E. Saxby . 1s. 6d.

Hard to Win. By Mrs George Cupples 1s. 6d.

Diarmid; or, Friends in Kettletoun. By Robina F. Hardy . 1s. 6d.

Johnnie: or, Only a Life. By Robina F. Hardy 1s. 6d.

Climbing the Ladder. By Mrs Forbes . 1s. 6d.

Jim's Treasure; or, Saved from the Wreck . 1s. 6d.

Jim Bentley's Resolve: A Temperance Story. By Lydia L. Rouse . . . . 1s. 6d.

Beacon Lights: Tales and Sketches for Girls 1s. 6d.

THE "GOLDEN NAILS" SERIES.

Price 1s. 6d. *each.*

Golden Nails, and other Addresses to Children. By the Rev. George Milligan, B.D., Caputh, Perthshire.

Lamps and Pitchers, and other Addresses to Children. By the Rev. George Milligan, B.D.

A Bag with Holes, and other Addresses to Children. By the Rev. James Aitchison, Falkirk.

Kingless Folk, and other Addresses on Bible Animals. By the Rev. John Adams, B.D., Inverkeilor.

The Little Lump of Clay: and other Five-Minute Talks to Children. By the Rev. H. W. Shrewsbury.

The Oldest Trade in the World, and other Addresses to the Younger Folk. By the Rev. George H. Morrison, Dundee.

Pleasant Places: Words to the Young. By the Rev. R. S. Duff, D.D., Glasgow, formerly of Tasmania.

Parables and Sketches. By Alfred E. Knight.

Silver Wings, and other Addresses to Children. By the Rev. Andrew G. Fleming, Paisley.

Three Fishing Boats, and other Talks to Children. By the Rev. John C. Lambert, B.D.

THE CHILDREN'S SUNDAY.

A New Series of Books for Young People.

Post 8vo, cloth extra.
Price 1s. 6d. *each.*

Bible Stories without Names. By the Rev. Harry Smith, Tibbermore. With Names on separate Booklet at end.

The Children's Prayer. Addresses to the Young on the Lord's Prayer. By the Rev. James Wells, D.D., Glasgow.

Object Addresses for Church, Home and School. By the Rev. A. Hampden Lee, Walsall.

No Ambition. By Adeline Sergeant. Large crown 8vo, antique paper, art canvas binding .   **5s.**

Schooldays and Holidays. By Adelaide M. Cameron, Author of "Among the Heather," etc. Large crown 8vo, cloth extra, gilt edges, with 8 Full-page Illustrations **5s.**

The Treasure Cave of the Blue Mountains. By Oliphant Smeaton.

With Illustrations and Decorations by Joseph Brown   **5s.**

Gertrude Ellerslie : A Story of Two Years. By Mrs Meldrum. New and Revised

Edition. Cloth extra, with Frontispiece **3s. 6d.**

Heroes of Discovery : Livingstone, Park, Franklin, Cook, Magellan. By Samuel Mossman. New edition, with Portraits, extra cr. 8vo, cloth extra .   **3s. 6d.**

Barbara Leybourne : A Story of Eighty Years Ago. By Sarah Selina Hamer. Extra crown 8vo, cloth elegant, with Frontispiece .   **3s. 6d.**

Witch Winnie : The Story of a King's Daughter. By Elizabeth W. Champney. Crown 8vo, cloth extra, Illustrated .   .   .   **3s. 6d.**

An Old Chronicle of Leighton. By Sarah Selina Hamer. Extra crown 8vo, cloth extra, with Frontispiece **3s. 6d.**

Mrs Romaine's Household. By Evelyn Everett-Green. Large crown 8vo, cloth extra. Frontispiece by Sydney Paget .   .   .   **3s. 6d.**

The Secretary of the C. M. S. Gleaners' Union writes:—

"Amongst all the many missionary works published we find that those issued by your firm give us most satisfaction, both with regard to interesting matter and to binding and general get up."

The Cobra's Den, and Other Stories of Missionary Work among the Telegus of India. By Rev. Jacob Chamberlain, Author of "In the Tiger Jungle." Crown 8vo, ornamental cloth binding, fully Illustrated . . 3s. 6d.

In Afric's Forest and Jungle; or Six Years among the Yorubans. By R. H. Stone. Crown 8vo, cloth extra, with 9 full-page Illustrations 3s. 6d.

Missions in Eden. Glimpses of Life in the Valley of the Euphrates. By Mrs Crossby H. Wheeler. Crown 8vo, cloth extra, with 9 full-page Illustrations . . 3s. 6d.

Korean Sketches. A Missionary's Observations in the Hermit Nation. By the Rev. James S. Gale. Crown 8vo, cloth extra, with eight Illustrations 3s. 6d.

"The absence of 'shop' from the narrative, combined with a sparkling and breezy humour and a fairness of criticism as rare as it is delightful, make the perusal of Mr Gale's work an unmitigated delight."—*Glasgow Daily Mail.*

Among the Wild Ngoni. Being chapters from the History of the Livingstonia Mission in British Central Africa. By W. A. Elmslie, M.B., C.M., Medical Missionary. With an Introduction by Lord Overtoun. Crown 8vo, cloth extra, with Illustrations and Portraits . 3s. 6d.

"Rarely have we opened a chronicle of missionary work so full of information, keen interest and encouragement, as the one now before us. Dr Elmslie gives a vivid, fascinating, and almost exciting account of what he has seen, heard, and experienced of labour for Christ among undoubtedly one of the most savage tribes of inner British Central Africa."—*The Baptist.*

In the Tiger Jungle, and Other Stories of Missionary Work among the Telegus of India. By the Rev. Jacob Chamberlain, M.D., D.D. Large post 8vo, antique laid paper, cloth extra. With Portrait and seven Illustrations . 3s. 6d.

"A capital collection of stories and sketches of mission work among the Telegus of South India."—*British Weekly.*

"Dr Chamberlain has given us here a fascinating volume, calculated to create and sustain a deep interest in missionary labours. It is worthy of a place in every Sunday school library." — *Birmingham S. S. Record.*

Modern Palestine; or, The Need of a New Crusade. By the Rev. John Lamond, B.D. Large crown 8vo, cloth extra, with Map and numerous Illustrations. Second edition . . . 2s. 6d.

Medical Missions: Their Place and Power. By the late John Lowe, F.R.C.S.E., Secretary of the Edinburgh Medical Missionary Society. With Introduction by Sir William Muir, K.C.S.I., LL.D., D.C.L. Fifth Edition, with Portraits. Crown 8vo, cloth extra . . . 2s. 6d.

The "Famous Scots" Series of Short Bright Biographies by Eminent Writers

"A highly creditable enterprise. The volumes are amazingly cheap, the get-up is pleasant, and the books published as yet have been eminently readable and trustworthy."—*British Weekly.*

Post 8vo, art canvas, gilt top, and extra gilt binding, price 2s. net per vol.

Post 8vo, art canvas, price 1s. 6d. net per vol.

Thomas Carlyle. By Hector C. Macpherson.

Allan Ramsay. By Oliphant Smeaton.

Hugh Miller. By W. Keith Leask.

John Knox. By A. Taylor Innes.

Robert Burns. By Gabriel Setoun.

The Balladists. By John Geddie.

Richard Cameron. By Professor Herkless.

Sir James Y. Simpson. By Eve Blantyre Simpson.

Thomas Chalmers. By Professor W. Garden Blaikie.

James Boswell. By W. Keith Leask.

Tobias Smollett. By Oliphant Smeaton.

Fletcher of Saltoun. By. G. W. T. Omond.

The "Blackwood" Group. By Sir George Douglas.

Norman Macleod. By John Wellwood.

Sir Walter Scott. By Professor Saintsbury.

Kirkcaldy of Grange. By Louis A. Barbé

Robert Fergusson. By A. B. Grosart.

James Thomson. By William Bayne.

Mungo Park. By T. Banks Maclachlan.

David Hume. By Professor Calderwood.

William Dunbar. By Oliphant Smeaton.

William Wallace. By Professor Murison.

Robert Louis Stevenson. By Margaret Moyes Black.

Thomas Reid. By Professor Campbell Fraser.

Pollok and Aytoun. By Rosaline Masson.

Adam Smith. By Hector C. Macpherson.

Andrew Melville. By William Morison.

And Many Others.

UNIFORM SERIES OF ANNIE S. SWAN'S BOOKS.

Extra crown 8vo, cloth extra,
Price 3s. 6d. each.

1. **Sheila.** With Frontispiece.
"The whole story is charming."—*Academy.*

2. **Maitland of Laurieston.** With Frontispiece by George M. Paterson.
"Her present story is certainly the best she has written."—*British Weekly.*

3. **The Gates of Eden:** A Story of Endeavour. With Portrait of the Authoress.
"We have not often seen a better portraiture than is that of the two brothers."—*Spectator.*

4. **Briar and Palm:** A Study of Circumstance and Influence. With Frontispiece by Ida Lovering.
"The author is as much at home among English folk as she is among the people of Scotland."—*Liverpool Mercury.*

5. **St Veda's:** or, The Pearl of Orr's Haven. With Frontispiece by Robert Macgregor.
"One of the most romantic stories which Miss Swan has written."—*Spectator.*

6. **The Guinea Stamp:** A Tale of Modern Glasgow. With Frontispiece by George M. Paterson.
"The interest is sustained to the end, and we lay down the book with sincere regret."—*British Weekly.*

7. **Who Shall Serve?** A Story for the Times. With Frontispiece by Ida Lovering.
"As an intensely interesting, well-written story of men and women as they exist before our eyes, this novel is to be heartily recommended."—*Scotsman.*

8. **A Lost Ideal.** With Frontispiece by Elizabeth Gulland.
"Among the author's most distinct successes."—*Bookman.*

ANNIE S. SWAN'S 2/6 BOOKS.

Crown 8vo, cloth extra.

Ursula Vivian, the Sister Mother. By Annie S. Swan.

A Divided House. By Annie S. Swan.

Aldersyde. By Annie S. Swan.

Carlowrie; or, Among Lothian Folk. By Annie S. Swan.

Hazell & Sons, Brewers. By Annie S. Swan.

The Ayres of Studleigh. By Annie S. Swan. Crown 8vo, cloth extra.

Doris Cheyne: The Story of a Noble Life. By Annie S. Swan.

ANNIE S. SWAN'S 1/6 BOOKS.

All New Editions, in Uniform Bindings, Illustrated,
Crown 8vo.

1. Aldersyde : A Border Story.
2. A Bachelor in Search of a Wife.
3. Across Her Path.
4. A Divided House.
5. Sundered Hearts.
6. Robert Martin's Lesson.
7. Mistaken, and Marion Forsyth.   In one vol.
8. Shadowed Lives.
9. Ursula Vivian, the Sister Mother.
10. Dorothea Kirke.   Illustrated.
11. Life to Those that are Bound (Vita Vinctis).   By Robina F. Hardy, Annie S. Swan, and Jessie M. E. Saxby.
12. Wrongs Righted.
13. The Secret Panel.
14. Thomas Dryburgh's Dream, and Miss Baxter's Bequest.   In one vol.
15. Twice Tried.
16. A Vexed Inheritance.
17. Hazell & Sons.   Illustrated.
18. Doris Cheyne : The Story of a Noble Life.
19. Carlowrie ; or, Among Lothian Folk.

The Story of Stanley, the Hero of Africa.   By ANDREW MELROSE . . . . 1s.

Jim Hallman : A Tale of Military Life.   By C. G. C. M'Inroy   1s.

Jerry and Joe.   By Sydney Woolf .   1s.

Fairy Greatmind.   By Maude M. Butler   1s.

Agatha's Unknown Way.   By Pansy .   1s.

Until the Shadows Flee Away : A True Tale of Last Century .   1s.

Marion Temple's Work, and What Came of It   1s.

Aunt Mabel's Prayer.   By Mrs Henderson   1s.

The Exiles of France.   By R. Hope Moncrieff   1s.

Robinson Crusoe.   With numerous Illustrations   1s.

The Daughter of Leontius; or, Phases of Byzantine Life, Social and Religious, in the Fifth Century after Christ. By J. D. Craig Houston, B.D. Large crown 8vo, on antique paper, cloth extra, gilt top   6s.

By Adverse Winds. By Oliphant Smeaton. Extra crown 8vo, antique paper, art canvas, gilt top .   6s.

"Elsie is one of the brightest characters we have met with for some time. . . . Mr Smeaton writes well, has considerable insight into human nature, uses Lowland Scotch as if it were his native tongue, and puts it into the mouths of the right individuals. The story deserves to be a success"—*Scottish Review.*

The Quest of a Heart. By Caldwell Stewart. Extra crown 8vo, antique paper, art canvas, gilt top .   6s.

For Stark Love and Kindness. By N. Allan Macdonald. Extra crown 8vo, antique paper, art canvas, gilt top .   6s.

Madeline Power. By Arthur W. Marchmont. Large crown 8vo, cloth extra   5s.

One False Step. By Andrew Stewart. Extra crown 8vo cloth extra, Illustrated .   5s.

Noel Chetwynd's Fall. By Mrs J. H. Needell. Extra crown 8vo, cloth extra, Illustrated .   5s.

Kilgarvie. By Robina F. Hardy. With Frontispiece by Robert M'Gregor, R.S.A. Extra crown 8vo, cloth extra   5s.

After Touch of Wedded Hands. By Hannah B. Mackenzie   .   .   .   .   .   5s.

THE PILGRIM'S PROGRESS ILLUSTRATED

The Pilgrim's Progress. With numerous Illustrations   . 1s.
Little Eddy Hill   1s.
The Young Artist. By Author of "The Basket of Flowers"   1s.
The Easter Eggs. By the same Author   1s.
Andrew Gillon: A Tale of the Covenanters. By John Strathesk   1s.
Jessie Grey; or, The Discipline of Life: A Canadian Tale   1s.
Sowing the Good Seed: A Canadian Tale   1s.
Tales of my Sunday Scholars. By Mrs Scott   .   1s.

The Lycee Boys : A Tale of School Life in France   1s.
Eaton Parsonage; or, The Secret of Home Happiness   1s.
The Race for Gold   .   .   .   .   1s.

Milestones, and Other Stories. By J. M. E. Saxby. Numerous Illustrations   .   1s.

The Story of Tatters. By Hermione

Livingstone and Park: Heroes of Discovery. By Samuel Mossman   1s.

Airlie's Mission. By Annie S. Swan. With six original Illustrations by Lilian Russell   .   1s.

The Bonnie Jean, and other Stories. By Annie S. Swan

THE STORY OF TATTERS

BY HERMIONE

On Schedule Time. By James Otis   .   .   1s.
Mr Leslie's Stories   .   .   1s.
Four Years in a Cave: A Tale of the French Revolution 1s
Saved by a Child. By R. Parker Graham   .   1s
Doctor Dunbar, and Elsie's Trial. By M. G. Hogg   1s.
The Red Thread of Honour; or, The Minster School-boys   .   .   .

Anna Lee : The Maiden, Wife, and Mother   1s. 6d.
Anna Ross : The Orphan of Waterloo   .   1s. 6d.
Katie : An Edinburgh Lassie. By Robina F. Hardy
1s. 6d.

Drifting and Steering : A
Story for Boys .   1s. 6d.

Joseph the Jew : A Tale.
By Mrs Scott   1s. 6d.

Juvenile Wit and Humour.
Edited by Dr Shearer
1s. 6d.

Bits from Blinkbonny.
Cheap edition, with
Frontispiece   1s. 6d.

Lucy Raymond : or, The
Children's Watchword
1s. 6d.

Bible Pearls : A Book for
Girls.   By Madeline
Leslie   .   1s. 6d.

A Little Leaven, and What
it Wrought .   1s. 6d.

Letters to a Daughter.   By Helen Ekin Starrett 1s. 6d.
Dunallan ; or, Know What You Judge.   By Grace
Kennedy   .   .   .   .   1s. 6d.
Rachel : A Heroine. By Edith C. Kenyon   1s. 6d.
Ruth Lavender : A Tale of the Early Friends. By Dora
M. Jones   .   .   .   .   1s. 6d.
Last Days of the Martyrs. By Andrew R. Bonar 1s. 6d.
The Orphans of Glenulva : A Story of Scottish Life.
New edition   .   .   .   .   1s. 6d.
The Magic Spectacles. By Chauncey Giles   1s. 6d.
The Old Oak and its Treasure. By the Author of
"Biddy"   .   .   .   .   1s. 6d.
One New Year's Night, and Other Stories. By Edward
Garrett   .   .   .   .   1s. 6d.
Pollok's Tales of the Covenanters .   .   1s. 6d.
Father Clement. By Grace Kennedy   .   1s. 6d.
The Exiled Family and their Restorers   .   1s. 6d.
Memoir of Rev. Robert Murray M'Cheyne. By Rev. A.
A. Bonar, D.D.   .   .   .   1s. 6d.
Little Bluebird : The Girl Missionary; and **Miss Graham's**
Protegs. By John Strathesk. In One vol. 1s. 6d.
The Old and the New Home : A Canadian Tale   1s. 6d.
Whitecross's Anecdotes on the Shorter Catechism 1s. 6d.
Whitecross's Moral and Religious Anecdotes   1s. 6d.
Whitecross's Old Testament Anecdotes   .   1s. 6d.
Biddy, Tibby, and French Bessie. By S. C. P.   1s. 6d.
By Still Waters. By E. Garrett   .   .   1s. 6d.

SIXPENNY BOOKS.

All New Editions. Illustrated. Cloth Extra.

Where Kitty Found Her Soul. By J. H. Walworth.
Captain John's Adventures.
Biddy. By S. C. P.
The Orphan of Kinloch.
Douglas Roy, and Other Stories. By Annie S. Swan.
Tibby. By S. C. P.
French Bessie. By S. C. P.
Two Gathered Lilies.
Little Fan, the London Match Girl.
The Pearl of Contentment.
The Pearl of Peace.
Robbie's Christmas Dream.
The Pearl of Faith.
The Pearl of Diligence.
Little Henry and His Bearer.
The Little Forester.
The Young Comforters.
Waste Not, Want Not.
Paul Cuffee, the Black Hero.
Fred the Apprentice.
Susy's Birthday.
Red and White Roses.
Little Goldenlocks. By Robina F. Hardy.
Nannette's New Shoes. By Robina F. Hardy.
Katie's Christmas Lesson. By Robina F. Hardy.
Tom's Memorable Christmas. By Annie S. Swan.
The Pearl Necklace.
Bess : The Story of a Waif. By Annie S. Swan.
The Bonnie Jean. By Annie S. Swan.
The Story of a Cuckoo Clock. By Robina F. Hardy.
Syd's New Pony. By Evelyn Everett-Green.
The Witch of the Quarry Hut. By Evelyn Everett-Green.
Our Father. By Sarah Gibson.
A Little Home-Ruler. By Evelyn Everett-Green.
Nellie's First Fruits.
Bunny's Birthday. By Evelyn Everett-Green.
Di's Jumbo. By M. J. M. Logan.
Dick : A Missionary Story.
How Daisy Became a Sunbeam.
The Little Sand Boy.
Jack's Hymn. By Elizabeth Olmis.
Little Tom Thumb.
Won for the Kingdom. By P. A. Gordon Clark.
Scotland's Saint. By James Wells, D.D.